To   Al

SOPHOMORE
SONGS

Hope You Enjoy !

Big Hugs

CLARKE **GEDDES**

Sophomore Songs

Published by The Conrad Press Ltd. in the United Kingdom 2023

Tel: +44(0)1227 472 874
www.theconradpress.com
info@theconradpress.com

ISBN 978-1-915494-56-6

Typesetting and Cover Design by: Charlotte Mouncey, www.bookstyle.co.uk
The Conrad Press logo was designed by Maria Priestley.
Printed and bound in Great Britain by Clays Ltd, Elcograf S.p.A.

PART ONE

1

The boat bobbed and thunked the gravel wall. The uncut, blinding sea mist was starting to lift. It was just before noon on a February morning, and expectedly cold.

Nick and Dominica, who preferred to be called Dom, set foot on the island together.

Dom was black, twenty-three, with fetchingly cropped hair that featured a purple streak. She also had a lean, very beautiful and somewhat chiselled face, not unlike a punk version of Jennifer Hudson.

Nick was twenty-four. His jeans had a few stylish rips in them. He looked healthy, yet also scraggy. He had fairly extensive stubble yet looked groomed too, exuding a dashing handsomeness leavened with an air of casual abandon. Dom noted a healthy tan for a Scotsman. A new look.

The weather was looking up a little, and twenty minutes at sea and numerous flights between them had left them a little weary. 'Pure as the driven snow,' inhaled Nick, mockingly. They'd managed to have a good catch-up, cramming in as much conversation as they could since reuniting at the port town of Auchsie on Sea. They had much to discuss.

Nick wore a knitted green jumper; he knew what to expect. He wondered what he'd do on the island, other than record.

'I hear there's a little pub on the island?' Nick asks the boat master upon leaving the bobbing ship.

'Aye, well there's only one. You can't miss much here,' he laughed, as he helped them unload their few bags. 'It's about a ten-minute walk along the Harbour.' He pointed along the waterfront. 'And all your music stuff is in the barn up on the hill there. We've been lugging equipment across fae Auchsie all week. Yous twa'll look like fish oota water here…'

He gave them a last wave and began pulling at various ropes along the side of the boat, hands wrecked in grease and cuts.

'You're a star,' said Nick to the man, in a slightly exaggerated Scottish twang. Dom, being an east London girl, still struggled on occasion understanding certain Scottish accents.

They thanked the man and his son, the skipper, and waved them off as they began sauntering along the waterfront.

The air was fresh and filled with salty sea fragrances. A creel lay strewn on the ground, flecked in brine and rust.

'Not like London,' noted Dom, cheerily. Nick grimaced, mostly. He noticed Dom had got herself a nice tiny neck tattoo. Nick always looked forward to the little time they managed to spend together these days, like back when they started the band.

The island slanted upward, like a huge upturned crater popping out of the sea.

'So where's this sound guy then?'

'He's meeting us at the pub. He's been here all week setting up. Don't you check your emails? And don't call him the sound guy, Nick. He's probably more famous than us.'

The pair chuckled, continuing as they were, drifting in conversation. 'Relieved there's a pub to be honest. Was starting to wonder if this was a set-up. Reality show…' came Nick. The minimal flight refreshments hadn't quite sufficed. Turbulence calling for another three mini Martells.

Dom paid little mind. Years on the road and in rehearsal spaces had made her used to his untrusting, self-deprecating ways. She found it quite amusing, for the most part anyway. After around a mile along the path, they spotted a small anchor hanging off a building roof in the distance, covered with some sort of lanterns and glowing lights.

'That must be it, then.'

They dumped their bags on the ground outside. Nick lit up a cigarette and inhaled deeply.

'What have you arranged then?' Nick snapped, looking serious for a minute.

'I've not had time to make plans, ok? I told the Big Man we wanted a retreat a while ago. But…' Dom trailed off. 'It's quieter than I was expecting, I know.'

They both stood on the street of sorts, cottages peppered along a walkway at the side of the sea. They knew where they were, The Far Isle, but neither had quite expected something so uninhabited, so serene and unspoiled. The quiet was almost unsettling to the pair.

'It's fine,' Nick said, stubbing his cig on the Harbour wall outside. 'We'll figure it out… Whose round is it anyway?'

They chuckled and crashed into the cottage-cum-pub, noticing there was no sign, merely an *Open* chalked on a board outside. They headed to the bar, with around a dozen bodies propped up in various shapes and sizes. Dom had made her way across the room, shaking hands with the lone figure in the corner, surely the sound guy, perched over a laptop. He had slightly lighter skin than she did, and looked a little geeky, with headphones draped over a De La Soul shirt. He had braids showing from the base of his hat, which she liked instantly. She pointed at Nick, who made eye contact, whilst approaching the woman behind the bar. This was a million miles away from their worlds, noted Nick, as a few of the men at the bar turned their heads and stared at him. On one hand, it had Nick excited, reminiscing about fishing with his uncle when he was a teen, growing up in Scotland. On the other, he'd suffered a slight anxiety attack on the tiny air taxi from Edinburgh to Auchsie, a squashed minibus with wings, before he and Dom got the boat across to the Far Isle.

'Hi there,' said the woman at the bar.

'Hi, erm, two large wines please.' Nick heard his voice break a little, unaware of the silent atmosphere around him until now.

'Sure thing, I'm the landlady.' The woman smiled, noticing Nick had now turned his back and was walking to Dom in the corner. A distinct smell of cardboard hung in the air, like a well-worn history let loose into the atmosphere.

He said a quick 'Hello' to the sound guy, popping his shoulder bag down before returning to the bar. Nick smiled to himself; he'd seen sound guy before, probably at an awards bash, looking like a fourth member of RUN-D.M.C.

The landlady watched them as she poured the wine.

'Fresh off the boat, then?' she said eventually.

'Aye we are. Nice to meet you.' Nick smiled, rummaging through euros and pounds in his hand. She reminded him of his mum, for some reason. She'd come across this type before. He was what she'd heard her daughter, now living in the city, call a 'Hipster'. He'd probably packed some vinyls for his stay on the Island, as opposed to a map. She observed the three of them again. The girl was a refreshing sight, thought the woman. An eye was covered with a streak of purple hair. She had a cautious look in her eye that the bar lady liked. A strength of soul.

The last week there had seen an influx of groups of mostly men, with American and English accents, coming to the pub at night. She'd presumed the men were walkers, or a Stag do, but soon learned they were setting up music equipment at the renovated barn up on the hill. The past week had, on the other hand, made her realise how long it'd been since she'd seen so many strangers.

Nick came out of the toilet and headed back to the bar, his initial anxiety of entering now easing. The lavatory reminded him of a trainlav from the 1950s. He'd seen the like in war movies that featured steam trains.

'What is he?' he asked the landlady, who was fidgeting with a TV aerial under the bar.

'Who, Dino?' She poked her head up. 'Ah, he's a German Shepherd cross. Best dog I've ever owned.'

Nick smiled and realised he'd be best to get friendly with locals. The dog meanwhile, had reminded him of an airport in Milan, being interrogated by the *Polizia De Stato* after his bags were found to be suspicious. He still loathed flying.

He winced and inhaled half a glass in one scoop. 'We're here to record,' he added, clearing his throat. He fidgeted at a nostril. 'Up the hill, in the barn?' He pointed toward their lodgings, which he and Dom had yet to see.

'I know,' she added. 'There's been people in there for weeks moving in equipment, and using our road,' she shook her head, giving a mocking tut, as did a few of the men at the bar. 'Never mind, it's nice to have some people here for a change,' she smiled.

'I'm sure it is,' replied Nick, sliding into conversation without even noticing.

'Is it Edinburgh?' she asked, and Nick stared at her, slightly confused. He paused for a few seconds. 'Ah, the accent,' he clicked, pointing slightly at his mouth. 'Yeah, it is.' They both chuckled a little. Nick hadn't heard her accent before, and although clearly Scottish, didn't feel to patronize her by asking much about it. It was very unusual, but there was an unspoken bond between the pair already, he felt.

'I spoke to my daughter on the phone yesterday. She knew all about your band. She asked me to send her a picture of you all, so I'll need to get one. She wanted to come meet you all, but I've not seen her for months. She lives off the island. She gazed towards the pub door as if pining for something, looking a little stricken.

'Never mind,' she sighed.

'At least you'll be uninterrupted here.'

'Aye. Well, I do hope so,' he replied, popping the three drinks on their table with his back facing the bar. 'Nice to meet youse too. Good to have found some fellow Scots.'

He plonked himself down at the table where Dom and the sound guy were deep in conversation already. He took in the room, the characters at the bar, mostly fishing types and workers, he thought. He realised, leisurely, how few people were around him for once. It had struck him at the airport in Scotland first, his connecting flight up North to Auchsee with nine other people on board. An odd enough experience as it was. Shifting between his anxiety management techniques, shots and a Spanish edition of *Rolling Stone* had helped. The pictures were good.

He'd been living in Barcelona East with his girlfriend, Ana Fazio. They'd been introduced by their European label boss The Big Man at a party on the last night of their tour. He also happened to be Ana's uncle. It had started as an in-joke between he and Dom, calling their label Boss, Mr Fazio, 'The Big Man', but it'd slowly become his nickname, not least amongst their group. He hadn't realised Ana was his niece until later that evening. The Big Man had arranged to have the band driven across the city. They'd partied with all of their label associates and PR people until the early hours of the morning, most of whom Nick nor Dom were completely trusting of. What did they do half of the time, anyway?

The Big Man, meanwhile, seemed to have an army of well-suited Spanish associates around him no matter where he went. 'Just another day at the office for the Big Man', the band came to often joke on tour. The phrase had taken on a life of its own between the two, inspired by their boss unwittingly. Perhaps it was subconscious, but if the two felt things were getting crazy on the road, it had become a funny slogan to throw around as their lives accelerated at a dizzying pace. Something only the two of them and their original drummer had understood since they decided to sign with Mr Fazio's label in Europe.

They had become quite accustomed to their life on the road, however, often not realising their cycle of hotels, flights and parties wasn't particularly 'normal'. Losing their original drummer and founding member a year ago had hit Nick and Dom hard.

Nick curled his lip and looked depressed for a moment, pulling out a Camel cig and rapidly filling the room with a stinking cloud of European smog. He'd noticed others in the place smoking, so no big deal here. Although deep in conversation, Dom noticed Nick's silence, and began to feel a little awkward, hoping he would try to join in soon. 'Do you reckon they've made some kind of mistake, guys?' asked Nick aloud, suddenly, looking at the sound guy and Dom whilst finishing his wine.

Sighs could be heard criss-crossing either side of the table now. 'This isn't where I had in mind really.'

There was a pause between the three. The sound guy looked a little uneasy, and raised his head toward Nick. They'd met before, he remembered, but he found this Nick to be a little rude, having spent a week with a team of the band's touring engineers to help set up their equipment perfectly.

'It's like fucking *Springwatch*,' laughed Nick. '*Weirs Way*' and all that.'

Dom was biting her nails across the table, rummaging around in her own thoughts. She too looked and felt a little tired out.

'This was both our idea. We needed to get away from the city. The Big Man owns the studio here, so it's a no-brainer. It's not a holiday…' She was a little disappointed in Nick's attitude. 'We're both burnt out. I'm not doing another tour until we have material, All right? Get the album done and I'll go to London and you can go back to Barca with Ana.'

Nick's leg was shaking under the table, she noticed, his usual ball of anxiety after a flight. The old dog poked its head toward the trio, then slumped back to sleep at the fireplace, now lit by the landlady although it was August. Warm in fact. The fireplace was cosy, covered with old trinkets and blu-tacked on ages old beer mats.

'OK,' said Nick with a slight air of resignation. 'I'll be more positive. My head's a bit all over the place, you know what it's like…' He trailed off for a few seconds. 'Of course the Big Man wants another album, but it's me who's got to write the songs.' He bit at his fingernail and couldn't help but laugh a little inside.

The scene had reminded him of one of his favourite movies, *Trainspotting*, when the gang set out to discover nature, only to be left swigging booze and at the foot of a Munro in the Highlands.

'Anyway. Thank God I already have,' said Nick and gave Dom a wink over the table.

'Have what?' asked Dom, confused.

'Written most of the album.'

This was news to Dom, although she was happy to hear it, secretly. Happy and surprised. Dom picked up a lighter and slid it around her fingers, the three of them locking into chat now.

'Nick, it's not much better out there,' she waved an arm toward the door, a few men were still drinking, keeping an eye on them.

Nick acknowledged her comment, although the sight of a fishing wader made his toes curl a little as he put his head up.

'Dom, I actually do like nature. In fact I'm sick of cities. The dirt, the rubbish, vampires at every corner…'

The sound man raised an eyebrow above his laptop.

'And I did tell the Big Man I wanted to get away for this album. Like that video of George Harrison, out in the trees smoking a spliff.'

Nick put his hands above his head, as though to make a bush shape, but looked more like some kind of alien impression.

They all laughed a little. The tension seemed to ease now.

'Are you on it, you tit?' said Dom, chuckling but part-serious now.

They both finished their wine, Nick returning to the toilet.

The landlady was talking to some men at the bar, having hopefully not overheard their conversation, thought Nick. Sound guy stared at his screen. He'd hardly spoken to Nick since they met. Colour bounced off his cheeks, changing continually as he peered into his laptop. He spoke now.

'It'll be like recording the first album, Nick. But as I've been briefed by your people, with less distractions.'

Nick plonked more glasses down.

'We need to be clever this time,' added Dom. 'Get album two going and use our time wisely.'

Nick felt they were both maybe a little mad at him, and realised he'd maybe over-reacted a little. He knew who the sound guy was. He liked his work. They'd met in Hamburg briefly whilst Nick and Dom were playing one last show in Germany, to appease the fans after losing their drummer.

'You've not properly met yet have you?' interjected Dom, although she knew they had. Nick extended his hand.

'I'm Cameron,' said the man, shaking Nick's hand. 'Cammie's fine,' he added, as though to make chat and some sense of Nick's odd behaviour so far.

'Or Mr Future, according to the NME,' said Dom, looking at the sound guy with a smile. He seemed a little uneasy at the remark, slightly humbled maybe. His teeth were powder white in contrast to his almond skin. Must be the American water.

'Whilst I'm here, I'm happy being the sound guy, or Cammie.'

'We met once in Hamburg,' remembered Nick. 'Oh yeah, you were with Mr Fazio and his niece. I'm surprised you can remember it, Nick' Cammie caught Nick's eye.

Nick squirmed, and then smiled on one side of his face, as he often did meeting new people.

'Yeah well, you know what it's like, working...' added Dom, glad the pair were hitting it off. 'You were both pretty wasted after your gig. But I knew Mr. Fazio, so it was OK. He's got a bit of a reputation with my guys.'

'Who? The Big Man? Surely not!' laughed Dom, as though they'd let him in on a little gang joke.

'He runs a tight ship, you'll learn,' she sniggered.

Cammie told them about his last week on the Island. Flying last minute from New York to Auchsee. His pronunciation of the word 'Aoo-ch-zeeei' caused a ripple of laugh among the three of them, not least the landlady. Nick changed the conversation to production. 'Great...', Dom thought, trying not to roll her eyes. She knew Nick took an almost obsessive interest in sound. Always had. She could see Nick getting excited and moving closer towards Cammie as they spoke.

'So what was it like then, working with Malkmus?'

She overheard Nick now, whilst ordering more drinks. She knew what to get Nick, hadn't even asked him. The landlady smiled at her over the bar, slightly puzzled by her scraggy hair perhaps, dyed purple on one side.

'It was...' Dom returned to the table mid sentence.

'Different,' interjected Cammie.

Nick was all ears now.

'He threw a few fits, you know.' Cammie let out a little chuckle as he said it. 'The Big Man likes to put me with acts that are a little, diverse…'

Dom remembered Nick talking about his hero, James Malkmus' amazing sound on a flight once, and she realised it must be Cammie's work behind his sound. He was said to be one of the best producers in the world. Known to squeeze every ounce of talent into a winning product, be it southern rap or indie-pop. Here he was, on a deserted island in Scotland. Cammie had helped mould Malkmus's distinct sound, and him being one of Nick's favourite songwriters growing up, the two found they suddenly had lots, and lots, to discuss. Cammie had made Malkmus' New York ballads sound huge, and Nick and Dom knew the pair even picked up awards together on occasion.

She realised he and Nick's conversation would soon become awash with mic placement techniques, guitar pick ups, and old amplifiers. She'd heard it before, numerous times.

She and Nick were still huge music fans, whatever was going on around them. As was Cammie, evidently. Perhaps even more so. Like a geeky production wizard beamed down to help them record that 'difficult second album'. Nick had always had an obsessive, compulsive side in the studio, and Dom knew this. So much so that they had racked up debts to the Big Man early on in their career, recording in Edinburgh, then Barcelona. He wined and dined them at the city's finest restaurants, in order to secure a European record deal. Nick had also begun dating his niece, Ana, early on in the band's tour. Which although pleased the label Boss, had perhaps put an odd kind of tension between them? They spent almost two years trying to recoup the money Mr. Fazio and the label had loaned them, but never seemed to quite get there. They'd struggled on whilst privately indebted to some shady characters in Barcelona. All of this whilst Nick had decided to whisk The Big Man's niece on tour with the band. It was an industry all right, and they'd learned the hard way.

Dom and Nick had grown up together, and she worried about him privately, his spiraling cocaine and alcohol use on tour. She was glad to get him away. Back to his roots, she'd thought. She realised eavesdropping into their conversation that they could be anywhere in the world, the three of them, and their chemistry and conversation would probably be much the same. The three sat around the table for hours, merrily exchanging stories of their upbringing, on-the-road antics, the various celebs they'd met. They picked up on how busy Mr Sound Man, or Cammie, had been in the last decade. He'd grown up in New York, helped hone the sound of many up-and coming hip hop artists in his teens. He'd then moved on to producing various singers from around the city, running three studios by thirty. He'd been recording with Nick's idol, enigmatic NY singer-songwriter James Malkmus for the last few years. They'd travelled the world together, and Cammie had agreed to work with Nick and Dom on the basis he heard something which excited him in their debut. A raw rock n roll sound, timeless but different. Hard to pin down, just like the first time he heard Malkmus.

They drank for hours until they realised Nick and Dom

hadn't even eaten, or seen their accommodation and studio yet. A studio owned by The Big Man and used by his artists on occasion, as well as one of his many personal getaways in Europe.

It was getting dark, and even the pub dog Dino had retired upstairs now. 'I'll be seeing yous!' waved the Landlady as they got up to leave, all three staggering slightly, their heads now buzzing with excitement, having made all sorts of plans for the studio sound they wanted to create. 'See you soon, nice to meet you,' said Nick, again becoming more Scottish than Dom had heard his accent before. 'Tell your daughter we said Hi.'

The landlady laughed at the three; one English woman with purple hair, rock chick looking but very beautiful. The American chap in a beanie hat and wrap-around earphones she'd seen lots of during the past week, with his entourage. He seemed to Joanne like a character from Waynes World, certainly not from around these parts. And the handsome Scotsman, who she had taken a liking to now. She felt to offer him a coffee and some fruit, perhaps.

'I will do,' she waved. She was still slightly baffled as to what had brought these three together, and felt it was all a grandiose fuss. Hot air perhaps.

'Put your bags on here,' motioned the sound man outside, clicking a little button that produced a pinging sound outside. They looked over and saw the sound guy hop into a golf cart to the side of the pub.

'I'll give you a ride up to the barn.'

He revved an engine of sorts, and Dom and Nick burst out laughing, for there was very little in the way of roads here. The exhaust popped and mud sprayed out from the back wheels.

They jumped on in excitement and the three took off along seafront, salt and sticky fish filling the air. They rode up a hill for some time, and though it was getting dark, they could see the barn outlined in the distance. A huge building more akin to a mansion house than a barn, they both noticed. The sound man cut the engine at the top of the track, now outside the house. 'We got everything you'll need in here,' said Cammie, getting out and grabbing a bag to help out.

'Wow…' said Dom. 'Well, it's bigger than I thought.'

The three approached the house and Cammie pulled out two sets of keys, handing them to the pair.

'I'll show you round tomorrow. We got work to do.'

He smiled at them both, all three drunk with excitement and glad they'd made it up the farm road in one piece.

'Aye, this should be fun,' said Nick. 'I'm excited, and free!'

2

Nick woke late. Disorientated, his go-to for mornings. He spun his head around and was greeted by a large window, a gorgeous sea view dead ahead. The room was bathed in sunshine, and for a minute he thought of his apartment in Barcelona. He gathered his thoughts and caught a glance at the little bottle of Valium on the dressing table. His best friend when flying these days. Next to it were the keys Cammie had given to him, and an empty shot glass befriending an open bottle of single malt. He felt tired; although excitement filled him, he couldn't quite put his finger on it. He remembered staying up until the early hours with Cammie and Dom, exchanging stories of the landmarks they'd seen, their favourite gigs. He and Dom had made their way to their rooms around three am, joking about Scottish slang terms and reciting them aloud. She was just down the hall. Nick had tried his hardest to get a signal on his phone, before soberly remembering there would be no-one to call at this hour. Ana? She'd be sound asleep in Barca. She was set to join them soon anyway, with Mr Fazio, and whoever he might happen to bring. Nick had recently come to dread these meetings with Fazio, which always seemed to end in talk of money these days. He inhaled deeply and caught a whiff of the linen, a fresh aroma of aloe vera and soap reminding him of where he was.

He remembered when the band had started out touring their debut in Europe, anxious to find a home for its release out-with the UK. Having secured a no.2 slot and taken the summer festivals by storm, The Big Man had wined and dined them to staggering degrees, paying for the most exclusive restaurants in Barcelona, in the hopes they'd sign on the dotted line with his company. If the Big Man had been involved in the band's ascension in Europe, he'd certainly dug deep to make an impression on the band. Little did they know it was probably them who were paying for it.

'Hey,' whispered Dom, opening the door ajar suddenly. She was wiping her eyes. 'Have you seen this place?'

'All right, lass,' joked Nick, in an exaggerated Scots accent, remembering last nights antics as they'd snaked to their rooms.

'Och aye,' quipped Dom, continuing the joke, but somehow sounding more like an Aussie farmhand in the process. 'All your stuff's here,' she said now, returning to her London accent.

'Nice one,' replied Nick, who'd spent his last day in Barcelona packing his treasured items from the flat. Records, clothes, plectrums and tech. Standard fare, these days. The rest of the main gear had to be shipped out of their rehearsal space ahead of time. The sound guy, Cammie, would be working his magic with a group of engineers long before they arrived.

'Have you seen..?'

Nick got to his feet and the pair stared out of the window onto a vast hill sloping gently down towards the sea. A picture perfect backdrop. Nick could almost smell the sea again immediately; a briny blast of sulfide and salmon. He could make out the small figure of a man, jogging up the hill's path towards the barn. 'Why's it called the barn? It's more like a small mansion,' noted Nick, aloud. On second inspection he noticed Cammie, racing up the path with a neon watch on, puffed out and pouring water onto his head. The pair looked at each other and laughed.

'He's keen,' said Dom.

'We should have joined him, maybe..' replied Nick, taking in the surroundings. They nodded in weary agreement.

'You've changed your tune. See you downstairs for breakfast then.'

Dom left the room shaking her head at Nick's desk toward the door, noting the addition of open scotch perched on the dresser. Nick smiled and let out a small sigh. It was a gorgeous day.

'Och aye,' he said aloud, to no-one. He changed quickly and grabbed a stray pack of camels, making his way down the hall's marble floor.

Everything was so clean, like a hotel. Quite a far cry from their rehearsal spaces in Barcelona and Edinburgh. Which although rarely used recently, were both pretty repellent generally. He finally found a door out and lit a cig on queue to the smell of the sea. He took in the landscape awhile. He gathered his thoughts. He missed Ana. For some reason he reminisced about the time she'd been auditioning for some dire Spanish reality show called 'NASA Training: Into Space'. Nick had met her in the city, outside TV HQ. Paparazzi had scooted by on a moped to snap her. They'd both found this hilarious. She had unknowingly become a C-List Spanish celeb in her own right, decked out in her LXN-EVO Sunglasses and ripped jeans. He pinged his cigarette under a bush, making a note to source an ashtray later in the day.

In the kitchen were Dom and Cammie, now changed into his regular hi-tops and baseball cap.

'Sleep well?' asked Nick, remembering Cammie hadn't actually drank that much last night, and was mid-sip through a bowl of green-coloured gruel sat at the table.

'Hey, yeah absolutely.' He took another spoon and raised his head to him and Dom. 'What? It's got spirulina,' he added, explaining his choice of breakfast.

'Yup,' added Dom, herself now heating the pan.

'A superfood?' Nick clicked on the coffee machine and pushed the button twice, hoping it would produce double the espresso.

'Well, we got work to do. My team left yesterday but we've got everything we need now, trust me.'

Nick could see the rest of he and Dom's stuff had arrived now; their favourite guitars, flight cases full of personal items and gear.

'I'll see you in the studio in an hour. I want to see you guys work,' said Cammie, who was obviously super-aware of their live show by now, but never mind. 'I like to get the vibe before recording, and I love the two new songs Mr. Fazio e-mailed me so far…'

Nick had used the last few months to write, even entering a Spanish rehab facility for a month after they left Germany. He'd written some acoustic songs, and already had a pocketful of older, unrecorded ones from the debut's sessions.

'OK, sounds good,' nodded Nick and Dom, now between gulps of tar-like espresso in mugs. They were both excited to record again, eager at taking advantage of some time alone as a band. No industry bods, no hype men, no hangers-on. Just like the old days.

It was a gorgeous day, and they arranged to meet in Nick's quarters in an hour. They both went upstairs and played on their phones when possible, and soon music had started up in Nick's room. He worked his way through his favourite tracks and records, from The Beatles to the Beastie Boys, a signed Pearl Jam vinyl Dom had got him for his twenty-first birthday a couple of years before. It could go on forever. Nick had slight OCD over his records, and would hate it if friends or visiting family touched it back in Barcelona. It was like a postcard to of all the places he'd been. Cities and landmarks he's seen, experienced and wandered over the past three years. Dom herself was a music fan, but nothing compared to Nick. He'd turned her on to so many great bands growing up in Edinburgh. Her dad was a half-Caribbean RAF pilot, who grew up in late 1960s London before being reposted to just North of Edinburgh. It was here she'd met Nick, a loner with a concealed handsomeness, and the two bonded over music instantly at school. She could hear the music booming down the hall now. Marvin Gaye, some orchestral pieces, Tom Petty. It reminded her of their college years, studying Art and Music, bunking off at lunch and heading into the city to buy vinyl and drink in the cheapest beer gardens, or listening to music endlessly over at Nick's. A small group of friends. It's also where they met their drummer, Jamie, who they'd hardly spoken of since arriving on the Isle. It was all still a bit too fresh, too raw. Like the stirring North Sea itself. He'd been with the band forever and was a good friend to them both.

He'd almost died in his sleep in Berlin, after they'd woken to the sound of him climbing into his bunk around 5 AM. He'd agreed to meet some fans the night before, just after they'd played a gig there. It'd been electric. No one realised it was their last as a trio. Nick and Dom awoke the next day to shouting and commotion outside the bus, and were pulled in at the side of Services on the U Bahn. The driver had found Jamie unresponsive in his bunk, having had a minor seizure. He was taken to hospital, and fortunately made it through after three weeks' recuperation.

He hadn't so much burnt the candle at both ends as doused it in petrol. Acute exhaustion and psychosis had caught up with him. He left the band two months later to study Geology, and was never quite the same. Luckily he retained some humour, and conceded he'd had a ball.

Nick and Dom made their way to the studio together, after a mid-day hair of the dog in the shape of shots of malt and a spin of Wings' *Greatest Hits*, which they both loved. They grabbed their stuff and passed a small swimming pool en route, a green-tiled spa ensemble in a big conservatory. The groundsman was cleaning the windows, alone.

They spent the rest of the day arranging all of their equipment, and discussing techniques with Cammie. Dom tinkered around on her bass guitars. Jamie's immaculate PD drums and a piano were set up, too, untouched. Cammie hadn't mentioned their late drummer since they met, which Dom and Nick had privately appreciated. By late afternoon, the three of them were starving, so hopped into the 'Bat Mobil', as Nick was now calling it and sped down the hill, narrowly avoiding potholes and a stray sheep, at one point. It was comical. They said their hellos to the landlady, who this time introduced herself as Joanne, and agreed to fix them up some fish and chips, one of two food items the pub served. They had more than enough back at the barn, but all felt the need for some air, food and some non-music related chat this time, if possible. Joanne served three huge portions of food, and after eating they all drank some more and headed back uphill on the Batmobil. Dom was tired, so went to bed early, leaving Cammie and Nick watching *Nirvana: Live* over the small cinema screen in the sitting room. They were all getting on grand, making progress, slowly but steadily.

3

'Who's there?'

Gmmphh.

'Get off me…'

'How'd you turn on this light?'

'We've got work to do.'

'Argh. Motherfu… Is that you, Nick?'

Cammie grappled with his covers and awoke abruptly, jerking upright.

'It's four A.M, Nick. Jesus…'

A phone torch lit up the bedside and Cammie could make out Nick, still clothed, in the dark. He was clutching a Martin Acoustic in his hand, by the fireplace. Cammie took in the scene for a few seconds, popping on his bedside light.

'Where have you been? It's the middle of the night!' Cammie said, admiring the guitar for a second, quickly piecing together the scenario.

'I've been downstairs. I couldn't sleep. Was out on the Veranda. Been listening to Leonard Cohen and Rodriguez. Anyway…'

Cammie wiped his eyes, shaking his head.

'I finished off a few songs, so… we need to record them.' Nick let out a nervous chuckle. 'I've woken Dom too. She told me to F off but I can hear her now. So get up man!'

Cammie's door flew open. The main light made a pop and lit up the room.

'You're something else…' came a voice, croaking and hoarse, but loud. It was Dom, half dressed in a ripped Vines t-shirt, one sock on and fisherman's beanie.

'Ah, Good Morrow mee Lady,' chortled Nick, in a cod-London twang. 'Care to join me for a snifter in the sound booth?'

Dom shut the door and let out a half-smile, shaking her head in bemusement.

'Are you high Nick?, it's quarter pas-'

Just at that Nick was across the room, strumming an upbeat melody Dom recognised. He'd played it to her before, on tour, and she'd loved it. She linked eyes with Cammie, who was on his feet.

'I've finished a few new songs, we've got to get downstairs. See you in ten minutes, OK?' Nick sauntered down the hall, humming a melody over the chords.

Dom followed his movement with her head and returned it to Cammie.

'Sorry, Cammie, I should have said. He did this during the first album. Stayed up till all hours…'

Cammie was gathering leads and such, wrapping them in circles. Nick popped his head around the door, unexpectedly.

'And the answer to your question my dear…' he croaked. '…Is aye. I'm fairly wrecked. Plenty more for you two gimps too. See you downstairs.' He slid off toward his room.

Dom rolled her eyes, wincing a little.

'Gimp?' laughed Cammie.

'Gimp? Does he know what goes on in my world?'

Dom let out a sigh, still half-asleep but laughing at Cammies attempts at ushering in some humour. 'Well, guess we'll see you downstairs, then.'

The three adjourned at the barn bolthole again. The house playpen for musicians to run amock. The equipment was state of the art, and a whiff of new plastics and felt was prominent. The band had always laughed about Studios picking up scents like sponges, as they hadn't been exposed to much air. Hence their rehersal rooms had taken on the unsanitary reek of alcohol and stale ashtrays, not to mention bodily fluids.

Dom had always been patient with the boys on tour, but even she would complain about the prolonged stench of earthy must and sweaty men.

Dom stood facing Nick, her trusty Fender Jazz bass slouched over her shoulder. She'd managed to throw on some jeans, and crack open a champagne bottle she'd found in the process. She looked rather glamorous, her pink streak of hair hanging sexily over one eye. She felt a little sleepy still. Nick was on a mission, now singing aloud toward the condenser mic. As Nick took a break he glanced over to Cammie, who was already set to record, other than one hand perched on a speaker next to his enormous mixing desk. Through the glass pane, he turned his back to Nick and Dom, crouched slightly, before raising his head back up, and puffing out his shoulder blades. Nick exhaled a puff of smoke, stifling the air-tight room. 'I had a feeling that's what he was doing,' said Dom, bowing her head towards Cammie. 'Oi Phil! Phil Spector!' laughed Nick. 'Just you take it easy in there,' talking to Cammie through the mic. Cammie rubbed his nose and began doing little salsa-type steps across his side of the room. 'I'm no gimp!' he cackled through the speakers. 'I'm from New York, Nick. This is how we do things.' He raised a small silver tray up to the glass. A mound of white powder the size of a golf ball was perched on top.

Dom and Nick burst out laughing, before Nick cut it short by strumming out the chord sequences again, making sure Dom was following the pattern on her bass. She'd remembered the song, and had pre-written an upbeat bass groove she sensed would work months ago. Dom listened closely, gently putting down her bass, zipping out of the room as Nick sang the song in full for the first time since sitting alone on the veranda. It was the first time he'd gotten past the second chorus, and Dom and Cammie stared through the glass in awe, their eyes fixed on Nick alone in the room.

It was just as Dom had remembered, upbeat chords but the lyrics were afresh to her.

Hope you weren't out there in the cold /
I learned later, your life took its toll...

Nick sang in the closing part on repeat, completely immersed. It was raw, very likeable she thought. Cammie nudged her, looking impressed. She glanced down and white lines were racked up on the silver tray. 'Help yourself,' winked Cammie. 'New York's purest.'

He had a slightly goofy look about him, Dom had thought. He embraced colour in his clothing often matched with a jet black leather jacket or ripped black skinny jeans. A slight air of almost childishness she found to be endearingly cute. She often had to remind herself he was a sonic mastermind, and would have every reason to be conceited, but he wasn't.

Dom went back to the recording room, suitably refreshed and ready to roll. Nick was listening back to what he'd just sang. Pretending not to look too involved, although Dom knew he obsessed over every last second of their recordings. She walked over and felt the need to give him a hug. He put his arms around her too, late, as if surprised. 'Nick, that was beautiful,' she said. 'Seriously.' He looked awkward, with a small half smile on one side of his face. She sensed he was upset. 'It's about Berlin, you know...' She knew he was referring to their time after Jamie's departure from the band. The meetings, the press and the stress that engulfed the band for weeks. Not least the exit of their soulmate, Jamie. He was in a safe place now, at least.

Dom thought of something to cut the ice. She knew the music was always a good starting place. 'Have you thought about the other parts? I've got a bass part, I think...' Just at that, Cammie opened the adjourning door to his stall. 'That was good, Nick. I can help with any drum parts. I'm a good drummer. Or strings, bugles, anything you want.' They all chortled. 'You know the intro beat to 'Get Off My Cloud' by the Stones?' Nick was working now. 'Could you loop me something like that? Just to jam to?' Within minutes the three were stood in front of the mixing desk, excitedly waiting as Cammie whizzed around his laptop and thwacked out beats with his fingers on top of his mixing desk. Dom could feel rushes up her spine now, and took a shot of champagne. She noticed trickles of sweat on Cammie's forehead. 'OK, can you practice and play along Dom?' he said. He dimmed the lights and a beat started up loudly on repeat. It was miraculous, almost identical to the 4x4 Stones intro Nick'd requested. Lights began to flash, and be it the substances or the music, or maybe both, the three had amassed a great atmosphere. Over the beat came Nick's chords now, not perfect, but more than enough for Dom to put down a bass-line. She plucked over them, the beat pounding louder now. Nick entered the room, giving thumbs up and wiping his nose under a strobe of changing colours.

Boom, Tick, Boom Boom Tick. Boom Tick. Boom, Tick, Boom Boom Tick.

It was on loop. The cymbals and chords came in simultaneously now. Cammie was immersed in his desk, but smiling nonetheless. Dom concentrated on her part, and Nick began singing again. Cammie sped up the beat, ever so slightly. Intro. Verse. Whoosh - and into the chorus. It was like a rocket exploding into the light. Cammie gave double thumbs up now, bobbing along through the glass. Dom could hear harmonies ping-ponging around her brain. What was that stuff Cammie had given her? Dynamite. She sang the harmonies into the microphone on the second chorus. 'Oooh / ooooh.' Then deeper. And again. Nick managed a sign to show he liked it with his eyes whilst singing. As Nick sang the outro Dom was getting to grips with it all. Completely buzzing now. Cammie kept the beat on repeat, and Nick's part.

Nick put down his guitar. He put his fingers to his lips as to motion a cigarette break. Dom nodded, but continued playing. This went on and on, Dom adding a bass-line and more harmonies. Sometimes recording could become like a factory-line process; do, hear, repeat. They hoped their live magic spark wouldn't be lost in the mix.

Opening the door to the outside, it seemed like another world. Night had turned into sunrise, and Nick lit up a camel.

Adrenaline, or something, caused him to inhale harshly. Other than being on stage, he hadn't felt this good for years. Cammie and Dom had stayed inside working, and Nick's brain was pacing at 100 miles per hour. String parts were coming to him. Piano chords in his head. He could hear the beat from outside on repeat. He stared back into the sun, the song now playing. He rushed back inside and took a turn at the piano. He stabbed out the chords he'd arranged in his head. They fit perfectly. Dom had joined Cammie in the booth, pleased with what she'd contributed. After what seemed like about ten minutes, in Nick's head, the room went dead. Coloured lights went out. It was like the end of a nightclub event, thought Nick. Like throwing out time. A little shot of reality came to him. He got up and joined Dom and Cammie, opening his bottle of single malt and took a swig. There was a calm in the room now, and Cammie removed his headphones. He sat back. He stroked his chin a little. He popped on an extra light by his desk and filled a glass with water. Dom and Nick waited. They were all hot and clammy. Dom nudged Nick and smiled, her eyes making notion toward the tray by their chairs. They took a bump of powder and passed the tray to Cammie.

'OK guys,' said Cammie. I'll be here working for a while, but here's what we've got so far.

They waited in silence. The beat pounded in again, like a rumble of horses. Their hearts were all racing, faster and faster, in time to the music. Cammie had added some clean tambourine strikes, and strings slowly faded in. It was unlike anything the band had recorded, but even in the cold light of day, it sounded enormous. They all made eye contact repeatedly, smiling. The chords and bass now.

'Reminds me of Bittersweet Symphony,' shouted Cammie. 'By The Verve.' He suddenly felt a bit stupid. Of course they knew that song. He got to his feet, as did Dom. She was over the moon. The vocals kicked in and Nick smiled. He liked what Cammie had done. His vocals sounded far more mature, he thought.

'I got some ideas for strings in the chorus too,' shouted Nick.

Dom was now dancing along, clapping her hands. Their straight-up rock n roll had found a soul. The song ended on Nick's beautiful outro. It was hard to gauge a song on first listen, but they all knew. Not quite what exactly. But it was near-on perfect. 'Before we enter into the finer details - well done guys,' said Cammie, relaxing now in his swivel chair.

It was hard to gauge a song on first listen, but they all knew. Not quite what exactly. But it was near-on perfect. Something special.

Recording continued until night time, and though Nick was eager to stay up, they were all deadbeat. They walked through the house and adjourned for one last drink, a toast of sorts. The song was complete. Of course there'd be obsessive tinkering by the band, but even Nick was feeling rarely satisfied. He'd managed to borrow a phone and had called Ana. Everything was fine in Barcelona; she was packing her stuff to come. Nick liked to know everything was in order, and it kept him calm. After deciding none of them could eat, they shared a lovely looking bottle of '97 Pinot Noir from the collection. None of them sure whose collection, The Big Man's presumably. It was delicious, they all agreed.

They chose their favourite records one after another, taking turns. Trying to out-do one another. Talk turned to the Big Man, how he'd made his way in the music industry. He'd always been a wealthy man, but rumour had it he'd made a small fortune in the late 90s and 2000s, producing super-cheesy European Dance Hits.

'Like the European Simon Cowell,' laughed Cammie, who'd lined up a #1 hit The Big Man and his team had been responsible for. 'Listen to this. You probably heard it on holiday in Majorca as kids.'

They all laughed as a synthesizer and a dance beat came in. 'Pure 18-30s Trash,' shouted Dom. They all fell into hysterics.

'Ana told me about this stuff.'

'The guys loaded though,' shouted Cammie.

'I might go down this avenue,' added Dom, swilling her wine and sprawled out on a couch now, laughing. 'Indeed. There's hope for us yet.'

The song ended and they were all slightly confused, although still laughing. It had sounded like that 90s hit 'Macarena'.

'I read about him on the flight over from New York...' continued Cammie. 'Interesting guy. His label went from producing this stuff to more serious artists, like Malkmus, The Tropics, and now you guys, I guess.'

'They're both pretty big on a global scale, you know?' Nick winced a little at talk like this, but couldn't disagree at their success.

He also loved their music. He didn't like pressure. He'd do his own thing whenever he could.

Nick and Dom lay next to one another on the couch, listening to records like the old days. They were both feeling relieved, and thanks to Cammie's input – and amazing cocaine - very optimistic. Although they were in very close proximity, there was no sexual tension. They were best friends, sharing harmonies to Fleet Foxes and Brian Wilson as they tried to get to sleep. Cammie had shut off the lights now.

'No four A.M. alarms please, Nick.'

They'd all done good. They'd all done good.

4

The smoothie maker was like a tazer gun to the brain, Nick thought.

'Turn that thing off,' he sighed, his leg slipping off the couch.

It was Cammie's turn, smiling across the room in the open-plan kitchen. Some con coction of carrot and spurulina soup, sloshing around the machine. He displayed an over-the-top cheesy grin at Nick, who was feeling sick.

'Morning,' he said, being serious now.

'I've made you one Nick.' Nick could taste wine, his mouth dry as a dessert boot.

'Cheers, I think.' He rolled over putting a cushion over his head.

'The pool's nice. Me and Dom did twenty lengths this morning.'

Cammie was hovering around, Nick almost expected him to break into an impromtu set of Cardio at any minute. 'Hats off to you, then. Bring yer goggles did you?'

Nick felt a pang of guilt passing over him. The sun was out again, filling the room with glowing rays of light. It was warm and comforting, and shimmered off the modern art pieces, which included an orange elbow, and a gun-toting bride, for some reason.'Here.' Cammie handed Nick a glass. He took a taste expecting it to end in turmoil, but conceded it was actually mildly good. A toilet flushed and out popped Dom, full of beans now.

'Ready for some recording then?'

'Dom,' Nick piped up, like a switch had gone off inside him. 'Remember the demos I wrote in Barcelona?'

She nodded her head. She was hoping Nick would get round to this.

'I got them too Nick,' added Cammie at the breakfast bar, a spoon of Muesli in-hand. 'I was hoping we could try and record them today.'

Before Dom could start up a discussion, Nick had already swiped the Martin from its stand. 'That sounds like a plan, I loved those songs I got sent,' Cammie agreed. Dom recognised the chords instantly.

'Hold on.' Dom marched out of the room, returning a few minutes later, bass in hand. She passed Cammie two CDRs. Nick was busy between smoothie gulps and chord progressions. He paused, looking at Dom.

'That's about five songs from the first album we didn't use,' said Dom.

'We've had them for about two years, but the recordings are solid.' Cammie looked intrigued.

'I'll be the judge of that,' said Cammie, tapping on his headphones with a smile. 'Cool,' added Nick. 'I wondered where they got to… Check them out when you get the chance, Cammie.'

They finished breakfast, by which point Nick had replayed the Beach Boys from last night, and they all felt good again. Fired up. They agreed to meet at midday in the Bolthole again.

Cammie was excited that things were moving quickly, and he made a mental note to take the CDR at every possible occasion, too. Just at that, there was a tap on the window. The three all looked at one another, as if stifled with a certain nervous, simultaneous fright. Tap. Tap again.

'Hello,' came a voice now. It was female.

Dom walked over and opened the patio door of the kitchen.

'Well hello Mrs…' Dom realised she didn't have a surname.

It was the landlady, holding a container in her hand.

'Good morning,' she'd replied.

'Oh, hi Joanne,' shouted Nick across the vast living room.

'Hi all!' she continued, letting herself in. 'I made some banana cake last night and thought of you all up here.'

'Cool,' added Cammie, now shutting his laptop.

'Thank you so much. That's so sweet of you,' added Dom.

Nick was in the kitchen now nodding.

'Take a seat, I've just made some excellent coffee.'

Nick poured out a mug-sized glug of tar-like Italian. Always number five in strength, if possible. He adored Coffee in the morning, even if it made him behave like a speed-addled Hyperpop dancer.

'Thanks Nick,' she remembered his name. 'I'm fine thanks. I've got Dino outside with me, he needs a good walk, you know, but good to see you all.'

'Thanks,' they all agreed.

They urged her to stay but she was happy to leave.

'Just making sure you're all still alive,' she laughed. 'Oh, now that I remember, we're having a music quiz tomorrow evening, so please come along. I'm sure you'll do well.' She was nodding excitedly. 'And I promised my daughter I'd send her a picture.'

'Sure,' added Dom. 'In fact, we could come out now for a walk, if you want?'

Nick and Cammie nodded, hoping to appease the woman for her kindness.

'Yeah, you can give us a tour of the place,' added Nick, putting on his favourite fur-lined jacket now.

He looked like a 60s Pilot mixed with Pete Doherty, thought Cammie.

'Yeah, okay, let's go.'

Before time, the four of them were heading down the hill on foot, not a Batmobil in sight, taking in the scenery and chatting. Cammie had brought a little speaker on his back-pack, the music adding an extra dimension to the walk. The Beach Boys again. Everyone seemed happy, with Joanne the Landlady acting as the perfect tour guide. She knew every house, every pathway; adding anecdotes about the buildings and their inhabitants. The sense of space was extremely relax-ing, a serene openeness seemed to charge the air. They passed her cottage now, the pub adjourned. She told them about the building, how she'd grown up there, taking the boat to school every day to Auchsiee. They all listened in closely, humbled and intrigued. Nick took the opportunity to light a cigarette by throwing Dino's ball a few times. Though he was listening, he didn't want to offend Mrs Landlady, so hid his cigarette under his jacket sleeve. He remembered he'd forgotten to take his anti-depressant medication, but never mind.

'Lets go on then,' said Joanne.

She led them along the coast road, the sun shining brightly as they all found themselves in a single file. Nick and Dom were behind Joanne, taking sly shots of malt from a hip flask Dom had brought. Cammie was taking up the rear, shouting the odd phrase in Scottish and asking inquisitive questions. Joanne told them laughingly how half of the Island was now owned by 'wanted men and tax evaders,' which transpired to be holiday homes. 'Wouldn't It be Nice' began to play. The sun was roasting now, and they all marched along the narrow pathway along the beach, the 'three Amigos' taking turns in harmonies as Joanne laughed at them. It was fun, beautiful. One of those moments Nick felt he would cherish in years to come, like crowdsurfing from the 02 Arena Stage in London, or having a cup of tea with Michael and Emily Eavis at Glastonbury.

They took a breath and shared out the banana cake, looking out to sea. It was nothing short of perfect. Even Cammie, usually immersed in some form of technology, had taken a seat on a rock and was taking in the sea view.

'Good cake, mam!' he shouted to Joanne.

'Thanks. Speaking of the Beach Boys, that's George Finn's house, further up there on the hill.' She pointed to a house, not dissimilar to the barn in size. 'I'm sure he toured with one of them in the 80s, or similar acts.'

They all smiled silently, they were enjoying the tour a great deal.

'Hold on,' said Nick now. 'Is that the folk singer from Glasgow, who made 'That's The Feeling?'

'Aye, that's Mr. Finn, you know of him?' Joanne looked surprised.

Cammie and Dom were all ears now too.

'Yeah,' laughed Nick, quite shocked. 'My dad loves him; he used to play his music when I was growing up! So did my uncle. Small world...' Nick was shaking his head, smiling.

'Great,' said Joanne. 'I know him and his wife Lynne well.

Want to see if they're in?'

They all got to their feet and followed Joanne. Nick was explaining to Dom and Cammie about his music, about a book he'd read on Scottish Folk Musicians, and its origins.

'I can't believe he lives here…' trailed Nick, still in a little awe. 'His first album is considered a Classic where I'm from.'

'Yes I've heard some of his music too Nick. He's a wise old man, is our George,' added Joanne, as if the two were related. 'Come on.'

She put Dino on his leash and soon they were headed up to the house, which was on the whole at a cliff's edge, looking onto the sea. Unusual in style and what may be considered a little quirky by some, it was impressive. Its character was a lot to take in, oranges and lilac paints weaving around one another from the outside.

'Wait here.'

Joanne walked down the driveway and thunked a round metal plate on the door, adjusting her hair a little. No answer. She waited a moment. Dom put her hip flask under her belt. Cammie had shut off the music. She thunked it again.

The door opened slowly, and a small-ish man appeared, holding a paint palette on one hand.

'Joanne,' he said. 'Well hello.'

He appeared pleased to see her. He widened the door and Joanne and Dino moved closer, Dino raising a paw slightly.

'Hi George!' said Joanne. 'We were passing and…'

'Come in, come in…' He moved back and raised a hand towards the group ushering them in with his free hand. 'I was just painting a new piece.'

The four of them entered the front entrance, before Joanne turned and stopped the three stragglers.

'So who are your guests?' George inquired smiling, as they all entered his living room.

'They're a band. They're staying on the island. So,' said Joanne.

'Great to see you George, it's been a long time. Over a year?' Joanne sat on the couch mid-sentence and ushered them all to take a seat.

'Yes, I was thinking about you the other day Jo,' replied George, popping his paint palette down on the marble table. There was a large easel in front of him, showing what appeared to be a band of horses drawn in painterly style. It was dark, moody and instantly striking. 'I'm terribly sorry to hear about Cameron, Joanne. It's just a terrible disease.' George sat slowly down; he must have been in his mid eighties. The three visitors sat in silence.

'Thanks George, we managed to get him to the city hospital, but…'

The three sensed they were privy to something, so all stared at the ground, unsure of how to act. They'd later learn that Cameron had been Joanne's husband for over thirty years. They met in Auchsee, at the outdoor pool. He was working as a Marine Ecologist, doing studies on the Island. Joanne was working helping her father out at sea, and covering the pub at weekends.

'He loved this place,' continued Mr Finn. He looked across the room, slightly sad. 'George, so as I was saying,' Joanne said suddenly, but in a quieting her voice, for some reason. 'This is Nick, Dominica and Cammie,' she said.

They all waved and said hellos.

'They're musicians. They're recording up at the Barn.'

Cammie gave a thumbs up.

'Oh really?,' George leaned forward, intrigued. 'That's brilliant…You know, I've always wondered what it's like over there.'

All three of them answered at once. Nick seemed to talk for the longest. He continued mid-sentence, '…owned by our friend Mr Fatzio, but really good, we've got all our recording equipment and instruments.'

Joanne cut in. 'It's the Spanish man no-one has met George, you know. The mysterious businessman…'

'Well,' she continued, '…He owns the house, and sometimes records artists there when he's up on holiday here.'

'Yeah I've heard that Joanne, Lynn keeps me up to date on the Island news.'

'So George, I told them to come for a chat. Nick here even knows some of your music.'

'Oh really?' Mr Finn looked surprised.

'Yeah Mr. Finn, my father was, sorry, is a big fan. I was hoping we could have a chat.'

'Yeah of course Nick, so what are you recording? What type of music do you play?' Nick and Cammie both replied simultaneously. 'Rock and roll,' Cammie had said.

'I suppose it's electric guitar music,' continued Nick. 'I'm a guitar player too.'

They all sensed they wanted to talk to Mr Finn. Dom about his art, which she was admiring all over the room. Cammie about his life, and music naturally. Nick about everything.

'Cammie here is from New York City,' interjected Joanne.

'Oh really, the Big Apple? So what do you play?' asked Mr Finn.

'I'm the sound guy, sir. Recording. But I'm a multi-instrumentalist…'

Cammie had a way of being very courteous to strangers, they'd learned, always addressing seniors with 'Ma'am' and 'sir'. Perhaps an American thing, thought Nick and Dom.

'New York, wow…' pondered Mr Finn. 'Yes. I was there in the 70s, for a month. A group of British musicians did a small tour. We met Bob there, briefly. It was an exciting time.'

They were all ears, Joanne was glad they'd been introduced. She'd known George would have some good tales, advice.

'I was like a fish out of water…' continued George. 'We didn't know Bob would go on to do so well, but we knew he was gifted, in many ways.'

'Bob?' said Cammie.

'Yeah. Bob Dylan. Anyway, we were staying off 57th St…'

They all made eye contact, momentarily frozen.

Mr Finn continued on for a long time, telling tale after tale, from every decade of his life. The 70s, 80s and 90s. He'd retired to the Island in 2010, leaving the cities behind 'For the tranquillity really, and to please my wife. She should be here in a minute actually…' Joanne had made tea at Mr Finn's request, and they all got along fantastically. Nick got to quiz him about guitars, Cammie about recording, reel-to-reel techniques. Dom about his art. They all found his knowledge overwhelming, he was a wise man indeed.

'Come here and I'll show you a few things.' The group got up and Mr Finn led them through a large cove in his house, ahead was a vast sitting room with a wall-sized window, looking onto the sea from high up. It was remarkable. Paintings adorned every wall, and five or six guitars were lined up. All three of them agreed it was their dream house.

'I've got a Martin acoustic too!' said Nick, taking in the guitars.

'Is that a David McClure painting?' shrieked Dom, nudging Nick.

'This is dope!' said Cammie.

They all stood and took their turns cramming in questions.

They could have stayed for hours and hours. The front door went and Mrs. Finn, a slightly younger lady, perhaps mid sixties, came in holding flowers.

'Hello all,' she said. 'Joanne! How are you?' There was chat going on at every corner of the room now, everyone being introduced to Mrs Finn, and Dino the dog could be heard barking at the entrance.

'So, everyone!' Joanne clapped her hands and the room slowly went silent. 'I'm sorry,' she said. 'George, Lynn…' Joanne nodded toward their hosts. 'Thank you for your time, I'm glad you've all met.' The room was quieting now. 'I've really got to get back to the pub, and see to Dino I'm afraid.'

'Yes absolutely,' continued Lynn, 'It's been great to have a quick catch up Joanne, come over anytime.'

The three of them were disappointed, but knew they couldn't stay forever. Nick had a sudden brainwave.

'While we're all getting on so great, I'd love to invite you all over to the Barn House.' They all exchanged glances. Dom nodded in agreement.

'Yeah good idea Nick, we'd love to say thanks to you all.'

'Mr Finn I'd love to show you our music things too' added Nick, trying to describe their three lives in a two words.

'We could make dinner; we've got lots of food there. How about four o'clock?' They all seemed impressed, to Nick's surprise.

'Tomorrow evening?' said Cammie, eager to show his interest too. 'Yes, well…Thank you, but…' Lynn was hesitant,

'Come on, please!' continued Nick.

'Lynn, could you drive us over?' George asked his wife, taking them all by surprise. 'I'm not really able these days but I'd love to hear the music.' Mr Finn stared out to the drive, toward a glossy jeep in their driveway.

'Yes love, of course, that would be great then. Are you coming too Joanne?' added Lynn.

'Yes, well, I suppose. I've got the pub quiz but…'

'Excellent,' added Dom as they all shook their heads. 'It's a date.'

They all made their way out of the house, each group talking to one another in varying topics of conversation.

'Thank you so much!' shouted Cammie. 'That was dope Ma'am.' He realised what he'd said, slightly embarrassed.

'Take care!' added Nick and Dom. 'See you tomorrow.'

They all got walking back along the pathway in single file, thanking Joanne and Dino, remarking on her banana cake.

'That was fun,' she said. 'I knew you'd all enjoy it. I hadn't seen them for a while either, but we're good friends. I know most people here.'

She told them about her late husband, who had gotten sick on the island, was taken to the city, but passed just eighteen months ago. They were all saddened, paying their condolences.

'But you know…' she continued. 'Cameron was my rock here. We ran the pub and had two great kids. Plus… I've got all my locals to look after, and they look after me.'

'Do you never get lonely?' asked Dom.

'Not really, lass. I'm glad to have the pub. We're a great community. It's important here. And in life. Remember to tell those closest to you how much you appreciate them.'

They all stood in silence for a few seconds. Joanne continued to talk about her life, peppered with words of wisdom, which they all found very fascinating in different ways. Simple some may have called it, but she was deeply rooted in ethics and morals, inspired by everything.

'Salt of the earth,' said Nick aloud, almost mistakenly, mid thought.

'Thank you Nick,' she'd replied.

5

They'd all left Joanne at the pub to organise her pub quiz, suggesting questions for it, to much hilarity. They ranged from The Spice Girls to Pavarotti, Burt Bacharach to Punk.

'Oh I used to like the Clash,' laughed Joanne. They said their goodbyes and returned to the house, back to a trio now. They'd all been inspired and had a good time, and adjourned on the patio.

Nick came out of the house, popping three wine glasses on the table outside. Cammie, with his trusty laptop. Dom, on her phone to her parents. They sat facing one another. Nick was deep in thought. Cammie closed his laptop, feeling he was being rude, and wasn't interested in his 10,000 e-mails momentarily. Nick opened the wine, pouring three large glasses. 'I love you mum. I miss you too.' Dom ended her call and sat back. She played with the purple tint on her hair, staring at it, thoughtfully. Cammie and Nick were happy to sit in silence too, taking in the deep Malbec in the sun.

'I think you've got the right idea Nick,' said Cammie, after a few minutes.

'Too much technology.'

It was so peaceful, nothing but birdsong and the odd comment. Nick lit a cigarette, passing one to Dom.

'What a day…' Nick added. Dom produced her hip flask, passing it round the trio. The silence was golden.

'It's got me thinking, you know…' said Dom slowly, exhaling the fire of the single Malt. 'I need to spend more time with my family. I get so caught up on things in my world.'

The boys nodded in agreement.

'Absolutely,' said Cammie.

He passed the hip flask to Nick, who'd finished his wine.

'Me too, Dom.'

He pondered for a minute.

'Tell everyone you love them…' Nick paused. 'While you've got the time. Not everyone is so lucky.'

Cammie glanced at Nick and Dom. They both stared into space. Cammie felt some form of tension. Not negative. Just something in the air. He glanced at Nick, and watched his right eye well up sharply. He didn't know what to do. Nick felt a single teardrop drip onto his nose. He tasted the salt, mixed with his Camel. Dom got out of her seat and pushed the table aside, finishing her wine. She crouched down and gave Nick a tight hug.

No-one spoke now. Cammie was aware of the band's situation. Everything that had happened in Berlin. He hadn't mentioned it to either of them yet. Nick squeezed Dom tightly.

'I'm sorry Dom…'

Cammie took another nip of the Whisky. He actually hated the stuff, but when in Rome… He got up and the three of them stood in a circle, hugging one another. Nobody needed to speak for the time being.

'It's been great to meet you guys,' Cammie added eventually.

'Don't apologise, Nick. I'm hurting too,' whispered Dom. 'You're great friends,' whispered Nick, holding in tears.

He felt relieved in many ways, and didn't feel embarrassed. They all sat back down, composing their clothes, stirring with emotions. Cammie thought it was time to say something with regards to the situation, and knew it was probably the best time.

'Hey. Yo.' He sat forward. 'Look, I know what you're talking about. I'm really sorry for you both. I'm sure you've had a hard time. I lost a brother a block from one of my studios in 2019. Some gang related stuff, three blocks from my Studio.' Cammie sat back. 'Life can be tough man…'

Dom took Cammie's hand. They all sat in silence again. Nick got up now.

'I'm sorry Cammie,' he added. He stood facing the wall for a few seconds.

'Toilet.' pointed Nick, explaining his leave.

Dom and Cammie sat on their chairs holding hands. The late afternoon sun was at its peak, ablaze. Nick headed to the toilet, wiping his eyes in the mirror, and put out a small line of cocaine he had in his back pocket. He took a pang of guilt. He inhaled the line up his nose, and breathed out. He felt more guilt. He usually did. He was high, but wasn't entirely happy with himself. Was there a light at the end of this tunnel?

Nick returned with his guitar, not his trusty Martin, but his favourite Green electric Telecaster. He placed it down. 'It's been an emotional day,' said Dom. The boys agreed. Dom and Cammie continued their conversation about Cammie's friend. He'd been recording with a rap group in New York, and two of the members had ventured out to a 7-11 round the block. They'd gotten into an altercation with a gang, leading in one of the two being shot in the street.

Nick listened in on their conversation. It made him feel

melancholy. All the while, he was also trying to remember the chords to an older song he'd written in Spain. He was used to doing this, listening to people talk whilst a melody played in his head. He'd stare blankly at the person, mid conversation. Chords or string parts would echo around his cranium as they talked, and he nodded, vacantly.

They came back to him eventually, but he didn't want to start playing aloud. He remembered he had wanted to add an organ over it, too. He had lots of ideas he wanted to try. Rolling, punchy drums. He was deep in thought.

'That sounded good, Nick,' Cammie's voice came with a nudge.

He'd gotten another bottle of Malbec, and shared it out. Nick took the chance to play aloud. They sat in a circle again. Nick plugged in the Guitar. Cammie had somehow found time to put an amplifier on the Veranda. He played the chords again. Nick wondered where Cammie had gone, but continued the chord sequence, over and over.

'Hey Nick, I was meaning to talk to you today while we're alone,' said Dom, taking the chance. 'I've written some things too, you know, like songs. On Tour.'

Nick turned his head. This was great news, but not news to him. Dom had taught herself guitar on their tour, steadily becoming a good player. She'd even bought herself a couple on the road. Nick hoped she had written songs, and had been waiting for her to play him some for over a year.' Brilliant,' he said. He knew she needed encouragement sometimes. 'Play me some... anytime.' Nick talked over the chords whilst he played. He didn't want to seem too persuasive. All in good time.

'I've spent a long time on a couple of them,' Dom said.

'I know!' Nick laughed.

Cammie returned with two or three microphones, and began unwinding leads and setting them up around Nick. He moved quickly. He was tactile. A man on a mission. Nick felt the effects of the alcohol now. Presumably they all did.

'I've been waiting for you to spill the beans about your break-up,' Nick chortled, going back to banter mode with Dom.

'You're not funny... I'll play you them later, though,' she smiled.

Dom had broken up with her boyfriend of three years touring the first album. She seemed to be over it now, but Nick avoided the subject nonetheless. She'd been single since, to everyone's surprise. Constantly fending off male fans and such on tour. Even entourage, as the band mockingly called them.

'Ok...'

Nick cleared his throat. Cammie had opened his laptop. Nick knew he was planning to record, but didn't really take notice. He strummed the guitar, and tapped his foot to himself. He began the song in full, with vocals. Dom hadn't heard it before. It hadn't been on the demos she or Cammie had received, which was mainly outtakes recorded from their debut sessions. The chords were striking, mid paced. A little like 'Talk Tonight' by Oasis, Dom thought to herself, nodding along. She could imagine harmonies in her head. Nick started the song again, before anyone could add any input. 'Can you turn my guitar up, Cammie?' He mumbled over the intro.

Dom finished her wine and took it all in. It was a beautiful piece, she concluded. Nick stopped momentarily, aping her behaviour with the wine.

'That sounds great Nick,' she and Dom buzzing.

'Can you try and sing this over the chorus?' Nick sang a separate melody to Dom. 'And then say *Don't* / 'She Go-Oo-oo* over the chord breaks?'

Dom nodded, 'Yeah sure.'

Nick started again. Cammie was fiddling around as usual. They'd somehow found themselves working on material, even recording now. It all flowed with ease. Cammie couldn't believe how quickly they'd managed to conjure up a song, regardless to Nick having finished it. The chorus worked amazingly, even the outro. Cammie could tell it was very likeable merely on second listen.

'I've got lots more parts in my brain,' added Nick. The three exchanged glances. 'Nick that's just…' Dom smiled.

'I love it too Nick,' added Cammie. 'I'll leave you guys for a few minutes to work some more…'

Cammie dashed into the house. He returned passing Dom her bass. Pouring more wine. All the while listening. Always listening. He made sure it was all being recorded. He went back inside. He went to the bolthole and gathered a few useful things. Another mic. Tape. Headphones. Tambourine. Cocaine. And lastly his slippers.

'I'm bringing home outdoors,' laughed Cammie, making his way back outside to the veranda.

Dom and Nick were deep in conversation. Cammie assembled everything and eventually settled. Dom had her Jazz Bass over her shoulder, plugged in too now. They played the song two, three times. Cammie had laid three lines onto a CD case, passing them around mid-song. He'd accidentally made them far too big. Never mind. They played on. Chorus again. Cammie sang along. Dom doing harmonies. Gorgeous. A simple, slinking bass line. They finished. A moment of silence.

'What was that Cammie?' said Dom aloud. 'A Himalaya?'

They all laughed amongst themselves. Nick ran through the song again. The sun was beginning to set, but it was still light.

'Let's keep going,' said Cammie.

They played it again, adding tweaks here and there. After playing the song perhaps ten times, Nick seemed to lose interest. He made reference to some other songs. Cammie didn't mind, he had a few tricks up his sleeve. He made sure everything had been recorded. He worked all the time, even when he wasn't officially working. 'What we've got is great guys. I've got about fifteen takes.' Cammie was back behind his laptop.

'Also... Nick, the files I got sent in New York. I worked on them before I got here. But they were pretty solid, man. I'll let you hear them, sometime.'

'Yeah? Let's go!' he shouted. 'To the Batmobile!'

Nick got to his feet and went inside. Dom followed. Cammie grabbed his laptop off the table. He guarded it with his life. They all made their way to the Bolthole. Cammie was explaining what he'd done.

'The recordings were good Nick. The songs are the reason I agreed to come. I loved them all, so...'

They entered the Bolthole, and stood in Cammie's lair behind the mixing desk. 'Hopefully you'll like them.'

Everything was moving quickly. Dom and Nick were licking their lips more often. Hot and a little fidgety. Hearts beating.

'I just played around, tidied them up. Added my New York touch…'

'Why didn't you say so?' enquired Dom.

'Cool!' added Nick.

Cammie slid a few buttons. He opened a silver box, removing computer pens and blank CDRs.

Opening his laptop now; 'OK, fuck it, I'll just play you guys the three songs.'

The studio lighting had come on, a mix of colours, psychedelic washes of patterns everywhere. Cammie composed himself. He turned, passing Nick a tray.

'I don't know how these weren't on your debut…'

Nick took a tiny blast of powder. He passed it to Dom.

'That stuff's phenomenal,' she whispered to Nick. She took a blast.

'Right…' Cammie sat down. 'Ready?'

They both nodded. He turned up the volume.

'I always said they should be on the debut…' added Dom.

A guitar echo cackled over the PA. Feedback, slowly rising. Nick recognised the song now. A bass line came in. More feedback. 'Just listen,' shouted Cammie. He took a blast. Guitar riffs now, in and out, playing with one another. Fret-boards flirting, cascades. More feedback. Nick and Dom turned to one another, they knew the song now. It had a huge intro, unlike their other demo, which they'd considered a little too thin. The amazing melody was the same. Bam. The drums. Like a punch to the face. Dom and Nick were nodding their heads, almost head-banging. Smiling from ear to ear. Nick couldn't believe it. It was the same song, but different. His vocals sounded great, not so tinny. It sounded like Nirvana to him, though the comparison would be big headed.

'Holy shit! That's ace Cammie!,' shouted Dom.

She sang along. Cammie put his arm on Nick's shoulder. His heart was pounding. He was getting good vibes. The next song came in, effortlessly. They merged together perfectly, almost like a song of two parts.

'I added something here,' Cammie shouted.

There was hissing and the sound of propellers. Cars. Nick felt a pang in his stomach. He knew what the next song would be, he hoped. Bang. The opening riff to track two of the demo. Souped-up beyond belief. Blasts of horns, a new, super-funky drumbeat. Cammie had done it. All of them standing now, Dom and Nick were dancing, but didn't care. They all held hands. Nick was over the moon with it all. His vocals were so crisp. Renewed.

'That's got to open the album. Both tracks. 1 and 2,' said Dom. She was overwhelmed.

'Hold your horses,' Cammie said. 'One last song, remember.'

The last track had been one of Nick's earliest. He loved the song, probably more than any of his others, but didn't want to play it live all the time. It made him emotional. 'Don't Let Me Down 31...' Dom remembered. It started slowly, a different approach. Cammie had stripped it back, slowed it down a little. Just Nick playing. All the guitar lines stayed the same, but Cammie had layered subtle strings onto it. It was sublime. Cellos, Timpani drums in the chorus. Violins. It was the best thing they'd ever recorded, Nick thought, thanks in part to Cammie. The song finished and Nick and Dom sat in silence. They didn't know what to say.

'Is it OK?' asked Cammie now. 'I took the third…'

Cammie was about to go into a dialogue, but Nick simply stood up and gave him a hug. Dom followed suit.

'Play it all again, Cammie. And the song we recorded yesterday in the middle. That after the first two. 'Don't Let Me Down 31' last.'

'That's it,' added Dom.

Cammie took Nick's instruction and lined up all four tracks together.

They three stayed up for hours. Realising it was 3am, time seemed to pass without notice. Nick and Dom had added tiny changes here and there, but as a whole it was their second album so far. Nick almost panicked at the thought of changing anything too much. Cammie's input had been priceless.

'I'm gonna call it a day,' said Dom eventually. 'I've got things on tomorrow. Emails. Phone calls. Reality bites… and remember we're seeing Mr Finn tomorrow.'

Cammie and Dom were still working, transfixed.

'Yeah. You're right Dom. Cool, I'll come with you,' said Nick, getting to his feet. They left Cammie in the bolthole, who assured he'd be upstairs soon.

They discussed food for tomorrow, feeling hungry but neither wanting to eat. Recipe ideas. Their ears were buzzing with noise. Nothing new. They collapsed on the couch, to a re-run of Countdown. Neither could muster a sentence.

6

'Banana?'

'Hmmm.'

'Maybe too sweet.'

'Aye.'

A long pause.

'Mixed fruits?'

Silence.

'I know. Too much acidity. Mixed berries? There's a bag in the freezer. Cammie's got half a market in there...'

Nick was sprawled out, ten a.m., sparkled on the huge reclining sofa.

'Red berries would be ace. I love cheesecake. Good thinking Batman,' replied Dom, plonking two mugs of espresso intenso on the teak table in the sitting room.

'That's dessert for tonight. I'll make lasagne for main then.'

'That's the best sleep I've had in ages,' said Nick, elongating his limbs, popping out of a shrunken Elastica T.

'I wake up drenched in sweat in Barca, look like a drowned rat.'

'Pffffha, nice. Speaking of which, you up for a swim today? C'mon, get your Speedos on.'

Dom cackled changing the TV from 'Good Morning' to 'Antiques Roadshow'. Nick got a pang of gloom thinking of Barcelona. He missed Ana.

'Is there any news about... the...' Nick enquired, Dom having been up before him. 'Yeah,' she said, rather upbeat. 'It seems to be easing, especially in rural places. Cities should be better soon. They reckon two weeks.'

'We should be All right then,' said Nick in a thoughtful tone.

They sat for awhile, replenishing their coffees, usually three did the trick.

'Here, Dom. Are you gonna play me your songs today, then?' Nick got serious between their mocking of TV presenters and cringe interviews.

'I'll do you a deal,' she brokered. 'Thirty lengths in the pool and I'll play you them.' Nick thought for a second.

'Aww fu…' he rubbed his head. 'All right then.'

They could hear footsteps coming along the hall, assuming Cammie had rewarded himself a lie-in.

'Morning,' he said, sheepishly.

He entered the room wearing his cap backwards, and dived onto the sofa, narrowly escaping a snapped limb on the table. He had curly, afro-like hair.

'Hey Cammie. You All right?' hollered Dom.

'C'mon, we're going swimming.'

Cammie straightened his cap. Different every day, they'd noticed. He flopped a CDR on the table. His face, usually able to escape his lifestyle, was gaunt. His jaw hung loose.

'I made you a present.'

He rolled his head back on the couch. 'I've not slept.'

Nick and Dom looked at one another, then at Cammie.

'A present? Have you been up in there all night?' enquired Nick.

'Cammie, what…' Dom was slightly concerned.

'I stayed up and made a version of the song. From yesterday…' continued Cammie. His legs jittered like a Monster-addled

59

acrobat. He cleared his sinuses and sat up. Shook his head. Stared into space.

'See what you think.'

Nick and Dom found this hilarious, cracking up. They were seeing a different side to Cammie now.

'Hahaha. Take it easy Mr Spector!' shouted Nick. 'Phil Spector here…'

'Jesus…' Dom shook her head. 'You must be tired Cammie.'

Cammie got to his feet, shaking himself down. He opened the DVD player on the TV, popping the disk in now.

'I've got my ways, sister.' He deadpanned. 'That's me on the drums, too. Took me a couple hours… used my brushes.'

Nick's new acoustic track from yesterday, out on the Veranda, started to play. Cammie had got a great sound somehow, very clean and clear.

'I cut up some lead pieces too, bass…'

Cammie pointed to the toilet and crossed the room. The bass line eased it's way in, almost unnoticeably. A drum beat started, akin to a shuffle, lots of snare rolls and soft toms. It was impressive,

'…similar to Alan White on "Wonderwall," Dom and Nick agreed.

The drums had filled it out wonderfully. 'This guy is unbelievable Dom,' Nick pointed at the toilet. He and Dom were ecstatic, hearing the song afresh with such new life made Nick realise how much Cammie had brought to the table.

'I'd love to get some horns on the bridge, maybe a Hammond or something,' Nick added.

'But it's… Repeat!' Dom shouted.

Cammie made his way out of the bathroom, filling a pint glass with coffee, chuckling to himself.

'Cammie that was honestly so good' said Dom, hitting repeat again. 'I love this song, love the drums too.'

Nick nodded in complete agreement, but didn't want to pass comment on his song. 'Man, I love it too. I've been drumming since High School, it's a cool hobby, I guess.'

Cammie took a slug of his Pint de Espresso intenso and sat down. 'I was gonna go to sleep but I'll just stay up. Hey, we've got half an album down folks…' he drawled like Lou Reed on a bouncy castle.

Nick realised he was right. Every track was not only strong, but sounded far beyond their debut. Not over-produced, they all had a blend and atmosphere though. Something he couldn't quite pin down. He had a reason for omitting the two tracks from his debut, he didn't want to play them live, but he was over it now. Cammie got up and grabbed his portable speaker, finishing his coffee rapidly.

'Let's go surfing!' he shouted.

Within ten minutes the trio were dive-bombing, practicing crowdsurfing in the spa pool, and blasting Dexy's Midnight Runners.

'Pass me that courgette,' ordered Dom, Nick happily taking the role of Sous Chef, having finished one of his only dishes, cheesecake.

It actually looked presentable, he'd decided. He hoped Dom's lasagne would impress their guests, taking any expectations off pudding. Cammie had thrown in the towel around 2 p.m, and gone to bed singing 'Come On Eileen'. They were both over the moon with his work.

'Hey, Dom. I was thinking today, earlier...' She was chopping onions now, her eyes tearing up. 'Do you think Cammie would ever want to play? Like, in a band I mean...'

Dom was a little surprised, and hadn't considered it. Although he was clearly a far better drummer than either had expected.

'Yeah? Cammie?' she laughed a little. 'I dunno Nick. He's got a lot going on though. Different lifestyle, maybe? Busy man.'

'Yeah...'

They both chopped. Pan. Chopped. Pan.

'He's so talented though.'

They both nodded. Chop. Pan. Chop.

'We can always keep it in mind...'

'Definitely,' said Nick, raiding the cutlery drawer.

'Hopefully they'll like the food. It's so cool they're all coming,' said Dom.

'Totally, my dad would be surprised,' continued Nick. 'I'll need to tell him, when I get the chance, but he's always on a building site.'

Nick was lent over the table mockingly inspecting the cutlery, piss-takingly referring to himself as 'Michelin Man' all afternoon.

'Oh, Dom, I've got to phone Ana too. She's probably been trying to get me.'

'How's it going with Ana anyway? We never really get the chance to chat somehow, these days.' Dom continued.

Nick paused. 'I've missed her so much you know. I've got plans for us. She's had a real effect on me.'

Dom smiled, as did Nick.

'Any word on when they're arriving?' Dom said, knowing

Nick never checked his e-mail, a pet hate she'd learned to tolerate.

'Not yet,' he sighed. Hopefully soon.

Dom had finished layering her Lasagne and began layering béchamel sauce.

'Cool, we'd better be on the ball.' Dom continued, and Nick knew what she meant. 'Aye, it'll be a hoot seeing Mr Fazio...' deadpanned Nick.

'Don't be a tit,' chuckled Dom...

'We're almost there. Voila!' Dom popped the dish into the oven, and in tandem they cleaned the surfaces.

'Hey that reminds me Dom... Look at the time.' Nick continued. 'Two fifteen. Time you showed me your songs!'

Dom had forgotten about their arrangement, but Nick had managed twenty dive bombs, and lengths, after last night, so fairs fair, she thought.

'All right, then. I'll meet you at the bolthole in twenty mins.'

Nick had to push the door open with some force. Cammie's snare drum and equipment blocking the door.

'Smells like Teen Spirit,' he said, opening the studio door, trying not to make any further mess.

'Phil was here... Phil Spector,' joshed Dom.

'Crikey, he'll be rough today,' laughed Nick, two empty bottles of Pol Roger strewn across the floor.

The two had been well behaved so far, not even realising they'd consumed only caffeine thus far.

'Got some beers on my way,' said Dom, possibly to aid her nerves.

Nick remembered where the lighting plugs were, so bathed the room in some soft ambient colours. Nick sat down on a stool by the mixing desk.

'Cheers,' they clinked bottles.

'So… I actually had some downtime in London, and…'

Dom put the CD on mixer.

'Did you record stuff?' shrieked Nick.

'Yeah but no, hold on Nick.' He had hold of the CD now.

'I thought you just had some ideas. Let me play it… Please?'

Nick was excited and popped it into the player.

'It's just me and my bass parts, some guitar, it's rough. I went to Rooms 2K.' 'Great,' said Nick, sitting back down.

Rooms 2K was a small studio in Brixton the band had used recording their debut, and still housed a decrepit band practice space. The song started up. They instantly had a different feel, swing, perhaps. More 60s girl group. There was still a swagger, a gritty backbone, however. Nick was intrigued. He could tell the recording wasn't perfect, but that was imperative, for the Wunderkind was fast asleep upstairs. Nick couldn't wait to hear the vocals now; he'd always loved Dom's melodies and harmonies.

'I've never actually heard you…'

The cigarette in Nick's mouth dropped down a little. He turned his head to Dom. He didn't say anything. Puzzled. Dom crossed her legs, slightly embarrassed. She began to blush a little. He hadn't been so genuinely surprised since the day the band got signed, after a rain-soaked gig in Paisley.

'Dom,' he moved forward, putting his cig down. 'I can't even concentrate on the lyrics. Your voice is incredible!'

A chorus kicked in, driving his point home. Moving up, and up octaves, amazing harmonies now, she sounded like Tracy Chapman, thought Nick. The second track was just as strong; faster, with more guitar parts, but airy and instantly catchy.

'First I've got to get over your vocals, now the guitar! You've really come on, Dom!' There was some intricate fretwork at play, but nothing to overcrowd the song. It was soulful indie-pop. Dom was swigging her beer rather profusely.

'Don't be embarrassed Dom, they're brilliant!' shouted Nick, as the track closed to feedback and rolling drums. 'Wow, wait till Cammie hears this.'

Dom got to her feet, suddenly.

'Thanks Nick, we've got to go,' she pointed at the clock behind the mixing desk. 'It's four. They'll be here soon.'

Nick downed his beer and got up, marching his way across the room.

'Aye, c'mon.' They power walked up to the sitting room, relieved the table was set and food prepped. They hovered around the place. Dom in the kitchen, getting a combination of wines from the fridge, Nick arranged the cushions and turned off the TV. He couldn't decide what music to play, so opted for his 'Acoustic/Bus' playlist. They heard a car pulling up the gravel, bang on queue.

'What about Cammie?' Nick panicked.

'Don't know if that's a good idea? I'll get him later…' said Dom, opening the door. She waved them in as the Jeep pulled into the driveway.

Nick opened the wine.

'Come in,' they said.

'Hi all,' said Joanne, helping Mr Finn into the house.

They all took in the sitting room.

'It's like a magazine house,' commented Joanne.

'Yes, it's very modern…' they all smiled, politely.

They got seated at the couches and Nick took their orders, two white wines and a hot water for Mrs. Finn, who was driving. Immediately Dom and Mr Finn had started up on the art. Nick wondered what they'd make of the Big Man's dubious taste.

'It's modern,' said Mr. Finn staring at a red canvas of burning petrol can, not entirely convinced.

'It's very unconventional isn't it,' nodded Dom. Nick downed a glass of wine and took the other two into the sitting room.

'Yeah, we're trying not to smash that thing too.' Nick nodded toward the marble buttocks in the corner.

Mr Finn burst out laughing. 'Indeed,' he wheezed.

It seemed to clear the air. Dom was laughing now too. Joanne now.

'So let me get this right, the Spanish gentleman is your boss, and, he owns this house?' Mrs Finn made a circle around her head.

'Yes, he is sort of. Mr Fazio is responsible for our music distribution in Europe,' Dom continued, reciting things as she had to her parents and family.

'He owns this property, and a house in Sicily, and Barcelona.'

'One in Chile,' added Dom.

'He's a man of the world, then,' said Mr Finn. 'Good lad.'

Talk turned to how they had never met him, but remembered the gossip when the house was bought, as was always the case on the Island.

'We've got some nice nibbles; olives, asparagus parcels and things. Help yourself,' said Dom, she and Nick bringing some bowls to the table. 'They're not fresh but we had to make do with the freezers I'm afraid.'

The guests all nodded and smiled. Nick felt a little awkward, clearing his throat. He steered the conversation to music. Or art. Anything.

'So you've got the music quiz tonight, Joanne?' Mr Finn said, as if to read Nick's mind.

'Yes, any input welcome, everyone.'

Within a few minutes they were all deep in conversation. Dom and Mrs. Finn had gotten onto Norwegian food somehow. Nick and Mr. Finn onto guitars and violins.

They all discussed Scotland, then America, then foods from around the world, reminding Dom it was probably time to suggest they ate. They all gathered into their seats, Dom having necked a shot from her trusty hip flask en route.

'Hope you all like lasagne,' she said.

Luckily it was vegetarian, as was she. They all loved the food, drank some more wine and were enjoying each other's company. The atmosphere was upbeat. Nick and Dom were relieved, Mr Finn even joining them outside after dinner for a cigarette.

'One a day,' he said, slowly inhaling. 'For twenty years now.'

Nick managed to steer the conversation back to music, he had had an idea out on the Veranda.

'Mr Finn, you've not seen our studio, it's a bit of mess but it would be great if you'd like to hear some of our music.'

'Of course,' he said, putting his arm onto Nick's. 'I was hoping you'd ask. Do you have anything with the Martin on it? She's a beauty.'

He was referring to the acoustic on the Veranda.

'Aye Mr Finn, sorry- George, I'll be two seconds.' Nick rummaged around inside. 'We recorded this yesterday,' he said, finding Cammie's new recording.

He put it on, and they all complimented it immediately.

'That's a very good recording,' added Mr Finn. 'It's not as rocky as I was expecting,' said Mrs Finn, 'The guitar's a little like John Martyn.'

Nick hadn't considered the comparison, but knew she was referring to the Scottish folk hero.

'Thank you very much,' he blushed.

Mr Finn had picked up Nick's guitar, and was plucking along. He was instantly buzzing, remembering how amazed and proud his father would be. They all watched on as Mr Finn played along, having picked up the chords, instantaneously adding his own frills.

'Amazing,' said Dom.

The song finished and a big applause went up. Nick knew he had to do it.

'Mr Finn, would you mind, after pudding, perhaps, if we recorded you playing along? It would be an honour.'

Mr Finn put the guitar down and straightened his shoulders.

'Well... If you fill my glass up, boy, I might.' They all laughed, Mrs Finn saying his name aloud, slightly put out.

'Where's your American friend this evening? Is he busy?'

'NO, no no,' interjected Dom. He'll be down soon. He's had a busy time lately. He's just napping...'

She fetched more wine and a hot water, and suggested they all tried Nick's pudding.

They all got to chatting and praised the cheesecake.

'Not as good as the banana bread,' winked Nick to Joanne.

Just at that footsteps could be heard on the stairs.

'Our friend's awoken,' said Mr. Finn.

Cammie sluggishly entered the open dining room, having at least made the effort of donning a new shirt. 'Hello my friend...' said Mr Finn.

'Hi everyone, I'm sorry I'm a little late.'

He plonked himself down, pouring a small white wine.

'Don't worry son. I stayed up for three days in San Francisco once...'

Dom, Nick and Cammie all burst out laughing, having to mute themselves, slightly shocked.

'You're terrible George,' Mrs Finn shook her head, then tuned away from him.

'Why it was your fault, my dear.'

They were all laughing now, even Mrs Finn. Cammie couldn't manage any food, but agreed to set up so they could capture Mr Finn's recording.

'Coffee, biscuits,' said Dom, as she and Nick cleared the table.

After dinner and plenty more laughs, Mr Finn again picked up the guitar, playing one of his own songs he'd written on the Island, he told them. His guitar work was superb, using a rolled up piece of cardboard as a plectrum.

'That's unreleased, so don't you put it on the Youtube,' he

joked, nudging Cammie. On queue Cammie had started recording, and played Nick's new song now.

Mr Finn again added some really nice frills, riffs, and had remembered the chords as if a natural. Nick was overjoyed they'd managed to pull off his idea, as was Dom.

They all agreed to head down to the pub for the quiz later.

'If he survives,' said Mr Finn pointing at Cammie.

Mr Finn cracking jokes and Mrs Finn thanking them all repeatedly.

'It's been a pleasure, an honour,' Nick said, more than once.

They said their goodbyes and Cammie, Nick and Dom waved them all off. Nick had stuffed a piece of paper into the Finn's hands with their e-mail addresses scribbled on it.

'Come round anytime!'

He knew he'd probably never see them again, but hoped he would.

If I can give you all any advice, added Mr Finn, having wound down his window.

'Sing from the heart.'

He nodded his head and wound up the window.

That was great,' said Cammie, after, having come alive after a few wines.

'To the Batmobil in an hour, then.'

He'd managed to find time to tape a tiny American flag to the Golf buggies' roll cage. He revved the engine, making sure it was still alive and kicking, much like himself.

7

'I didn't cheat, I'm an American!' shouted Cammie across the sitting room, flicking Nick and Dom the V's, laughing out loud. They'd been irked since they got up, having faced defeat at the pub music quiz. It'd been a close race, Nick and Dom deciding to pair up whilst Cammie went it alone. The finale had been a two way tie break, a local cultivator losing out last minute, having had an unforeseen knowledge of 80s Pop Hits.

'My knowledge of Sugarhill Gang is strong, I'm afraid…' mused Cammie.

The three had again evaded injury on the Batmobil coming home, and had had a good laugh with some of the locals and Joanne. It'd been a sensible night overall, Cammie discovering a love for pork scratchings and Guinness. They were all in bed by long before sunrise.

They'd decided to do their own thing in the morning, meet for a decent lunch and then more recording. Cammie and Dom had their bursting inboxes to attend, almost demolishing a box of nutty muesli along the way. Nick, having left his socials and band website to Dom around a year ago, kept it simple by calling his Dad and Ana, who were both glad to hear from him. His dad had been shocked to hear Mr Finn not only lived on the Island, but would maybe even make it onto their new album, had the recording been a success.

Ana was well too, excitedly waiting to see the place, and Nick. It would be her first time in Scotland.

She told Nick Papi had been in Chile, but they would all fly out when he returned to Barca. Papi was Ana's name for the Big Man, her Uncle, so Nick knew whom she was referring to.

'I love you,' she said lastly, Nick's heart skipping a beat.

'I love you too Ana, I know I haven't said it enough.'

Nick felt a bit sombre hanging up, he'd never felt so engulfed by anyone. He returned to his room to hunt for his 200 Marlborough, and decided to play around with his guitars, maybe write some more. He'd actually had around nine or ten new songs written acoustically, so decided to play them later to Dom and Cammie, maybe like a set of new songs. He grabbed his Telecaster and got to work.

'First pork scratchings and now this?' said Cammie, tasting the cauliflower steak and beans Dom had made them for lunch. He seemed to like them, and was always quizzing Dom about veggie foods and tips.

'I gotta try a Scottish pie sometime though,' Cammie had said, with fish and chips off the bucket list now, thanks to Joanne at the Pub.

'And what's that orange soda stuff? Looks like ginger hair?'

They all laughed, eventually realising it was Irn Bru.

'So Dom, Nick kept telling me about your songs yeah? I gotta hear them too. That's great…'

Dom wasn't too keen on the idea, but they both insisted.

'Just wait,' said Nick, handing out some beers. 'Also, I was going to do a little gig for you guys? I've got about nine songs to play you, Ana was helping me chose them on the phone. Then we can see what ones we want to use.'

Nick and Dom were surprised, and they all headed to the bolthole as soon as possible. Dom had brought her hip flask, Cammie his slippers, bath robe and shades. They were still discussing Scottish foods, explaining Haggis to Cammie, who didn't seem to enthusiastic, contorting his face at it.

'Burns Night? Like in a fire?'

They gave the Studio a quick spruce and Nick arranged his set-up.

'Hopefully I'll remember them all,' said Nick, through the condenser mic to Cammie's lair.

'We're all set on this side,' Cammie said, himself and Dom getting comfortable. 'Should have brought some popcorn,' said Dom with a smile.

For the next hour or so Nick treated them to a meticulously remembered set of new songs. Neither had heard any before, talking amongst themselves between songs.

It was hard to gauge on first listen, so Cammie managed to persuade Nick to run through them all again. And again. He'd been scribbling notes here and there, making Nick a little uncomfortable, teasingly saying 'four out of ten' and 'I hope that's not about Irn Bru' through the tannoy.

Cammie had recorded them all to replay throughout the day, and planned to do the same with Dom's tracks. Dom was content, enjoying the experience, and couldn't wait to hear them recorded. She had lots of ideas for harmonies, mainly, but also Bass parts and other instruments. As did Nick, as always, and Cammie.

'That's a strong set of songs Nick,' noted Cammie as he made his way back to the lair.

'I think I've got five I'd really like to record,' said Nick now.

They all agreed on his choices, the direction they could go, which ones would be great as 'Punchy Indie nuggets' as Cammie put it, and which Nick wanted to keep stripped-back, maybe even acoustic.

They hadn't intended to do so, but what started off as Nick playing some new songs turned into a Jam, with Cammie happily agreeing to play drums to help the songs take structure. He was a solid drummer with his own style, adaptive on slower songs, and more than capable of morphing into straight-up, Nirvavna-era Dave Grohl when necessary. He also knew better than most how to structure Nick's songs, often suggesting harmonies and bridge parts be re-arranged. Dom too, grew to love Cammie's ear, deeply intuitive to all of her Bass parts. She'd agreed to play him her two song demo, which he loved, as Nick expected. Her voice was different on a full recording, Cammie urging her to sing a lot more often, as opposed to just harmonies on Nick's tracks. They played around with the songs, Cammie comparing them to the Raveonettes, and he played them relentlessly on the drums, eventually live as a three piece between Nick's songs. The songs gelled together so well, as did Nick, Dom and Cammie. They couldn't imagine writing and recording with anyone else again.

They drank beers, shared anecdotes, having built their own lingo and indecipherable humour between them. Nine hours turned to fifteen, stopping for food, shots, and showers. Fifteen hours to twenty two. Their ears, limbs and brainpower had been sucked dry. They were exhausted. But they'd made huge progress.

Dom managed to get revenge on Cammie by cracking jokes about Twinkies, Poop on a Shingle and Beef Jerky along the way. They all collapsed watching Whiplash in the sitting room, content but not finished.

'I thought I said ten. So sorry.'

Dom had awoken to her phone ringing. 9 a.m. Nick and Cammie stirred on the couch. She'd forgotten she'd agreed to a morning of calls to a handful of Magazines and Websites, beginning with The Wire, who wanted an update on the album and recording. She managed to gather her shoes and slid out the patio doors, popping the coffee machine on in the process. Nick and Cammie woke eventually, checking the date on the kitchen calendar, enjoying mugs of deepest black espresso; waving and pulling moonies at Dom, who was deep in conversation on the Veranda. She returned the favour by shaking her wrist at the pair.

They headed outside to bring her a coffee, and eavesdrop, which quickly descended into making a mockery when possible.

'No it's not a retreat. We've been really busy. It's a different life for us all, momentarily.' Cammie held up an empty can of beer, whilst Nick posed with a guitar between his legs on top of the barbecue. 'Yes Cameron. He's been an amazing producer so far. His techniques are so... unorthodox.'

Dom held the phone, trying to be serious, sticking a middle finger up to the pair mid sentence. They agreed enough was enough, and headed inside to work on Dom's songs and recordings by way of an apology. Nick felt a little guilty, but Dom had agreed to take control of the bands press and what not whilst not on tour, and was happy to do so.

'OK, let's work...'

The pair worked on the songs with fresh ears, hyped to hopefully finish them up soon. The recordings were solid, it was just a case of them all adding any input where they felt necessary. Dom joined them after a couple of hours, looking impressed by everything she heard. She and Nick had changed dynamics, she supposed, her being the main input on these tracks. Other than hoping to try out some tambourine and possibly some subtle horns, she couldn't hear any way they could be improved.

They all decided to pop a bottle of Cammie's champagne to celebrate, listening to the seven finished tracks on repeat a couple of times, discussing which songs so far would fit where.

'Track eight has to be great, it's an unwritten rule,' said Nick, and they both agreed. 'I'm a little fed up of the openers all being the singles,' he added, however he had to reconsider after talk of the label not being happy was raised.

'Tell it to the Big Man,' joked Dom.

'Hey speaking of Mr Fazio, I got an e-mail at lunchtime from my guys in New York,' said Cammie, Nick and Dom all ears. 'He's coming with his people on Sunday.' 'This Sunday?' they enquired, slightly alarmed.

'Yeah. Sunday or Monday, so we'd better remember...'

It was mostly good news, Nick excited to see Ana, but nothing was said about Mr Fazio coming. They worked until late afternoon and concurred a studio break might do them good for a couple of hours. Nick had wanted to visit a converted lighthouse on the far side of the Island, and Cammie and Dom both agreed. They opted for the Batmobil, which was slowly garnering a few souvenirs, trinkets and flags by now. Luckily it was still in one piece, and they climbed aboard taking a small picnic of champagne, olives and sorbet from the kitchen.

Nick managed to tape his speaker to his side of the frame, so they bobbed around the island listening to Shine Vol. 5 for a bit, waving at the postman and chatting to a local deckhand about his new Fender Jaguar. He also showed them the route to the lighthouse, before his frosty geese chased the Golf Buggy off the drive. They arrived just by sunset, and it was a lovely view. Along the ridged coastline sat a solitary bench overlooking the sea and the lighthouse. They opened the champagne, shared the food and took in the surroundings.

'Hey Cammie, how come you never joined a band anyway?' asked Dom, as talk moved from football hooliganism to drummers, for some reason.

'I never got the chance, you know. After high school I was in the studio non-stop. First with my uncle Ray. Then for a rap label in Hudson. Then back to NY on my own shit. Nowadays I pick who I wanna work with. It's the dream. Why, you hiring?'

He chuckled a little, continuing his story about his uncle once pre-rolling fifty blunts for a visiting hip-hop collective.

'Yeah we are, hiring I guess,' said Nick, catching his eye, '... so if you ever wanted to consider it.'

There was a tiny pause, before Dom changed the subject

back to the fifty blunt fiasco. 'Yeah?' said Cammie, now totally unsure of what to say.

He'd never considered joining their band. He was the sound guy. The record producer. He'd done it for fifteen years.

'Uhm…can I think about it?'

'Yeah, course,' they both replied, 'It'd be a different life, I know but, you're a fantastic musician,' said Nick. 'And a dear friend now too. Like one of the band.'

Cammie felt lucky, but didn't know what to think or say.

'Cool. I'll give it some thought. I love this new record man. I told my man on the phone today. Shit's different.'

'A toast,' said Nick, and they all clinked glasses, before talk turned to the pros and cons of living in a lighthouse awhile.

Cammie's new adoration for Guinness called for a pit stop at the Pub, so they weaved back there for some fish and chips, with Joanne surprisingly joining them for tea, before another six hours of recording and mixing.

Nick and Dom had finished up their food, Joanne having supplied some excess homemade tartar sauce. They were all stuffed and sprawled out on their small stools by the fire.

'Flavio helped me,' she waived a finger towards the bar. A middle aged man caught their eye but didn't return any pleasantries. 'With the gherkins, for the sauce. He's a dab hand in the old allotment. He's been here for ten days or so, working on organic farms or something, they call it. He's a bit, maybe shy, I'd say. I thought he was a wee bit simple, perhaps.' Joanne had hushed her voice a little.

Dom took in the man as she spoke, having almost presumed

he was romantically involved with Joanne. He had graying jet-black hair, very unshaven, torn at the base trousers and a natty plaid shirt. He hadn't spoken to anyone in the place since they arrived.

'He can come over and join us, no?' queried Nick, almost feeling a little sorry for the man. He looked like he needed some TLC. A warm bath, perhaps. Though he didn't come across very approachable, from his demeanor.

'It's fine. His English is very limited. He speaks some Slavic languages; I think he was born in Serbia. But no fixed abode if you ken what I mean. I tell you though; he can sure use an axe.' She hushed her voice further. 'I caught him putting in false teeth the other day. Poor soul must only be in his thirties. Anyway, he potters around the place. It's fine for me for a couple of months.'

The man stood up and flicked a stray peanut back into a tin cup at the bar. He roughly inhaled a ball of phlegm up a nostril. He muttered something foreign to himself, took a rapid double nip of Malt and walked out the door. Dom caught sight of his eyes on the way out; a cold, unsettling stare and a raised left lip. He looked furious. She flicked her purple behind her ear, as she often did when edgy, and wrinkled her forehead. The pub door banged shut. *Rude man*, she thought.

'Anyway, as I was saying, the tartare sauce has been a hit. You better get back up the road and record some hits, no?'

The album was taking shape, slowly but surely. After a tedious but essential mixing session and much discussion, they finally agreed on what movie to watch, with Dom's suggestion of The Alpinist winning out.

8

'Don't quote me on this, but it's supposed to be the Ultimate Breakfast.'

Cammie was at it again, eight thirty now, making his trademark smoothies.

'We got a double shot of ginger, spurulina, carrot, orange, flaxseed, and spinach.' 'Spinach?' said Nick, raising an eyebrow.

'Wow, I'm inspired,' said Dom, as the machine blitzed and whirred now.

Truth be told they both loved Cammie's morning medicines by now, often discussing different combinations for the Ultimate Getup Gruel. Nick had gotten used to a jug of espresso, washed down with anti-depressants and the occasionally croissant de almendra from Lucas Café across the street.

'I'm gonna keep this up you know,' he said.

'We'll need to you to come on tour Cammie. Mr Motivator.'

He'd meant the comment an offhand joke, but it seemed he was only half joking.

'So Nick, are you happy with the four new songs we decided on then, from your set?'

They'd been practicing Nick's new songs for hours last night, all of them deemed the best from his set of nine. He'd completely agreed.

'Paired with the tracks we already have, and Dom's hidden gems, we've got a solid album coming here, guys. No question. I can honestly say I'm happy with it already. Sure I want to try this or that, but overall…' Nick shook his head up and down. 'It's all sounding better than the first.'

'Definitely,' added Dom.

'But, are you ready?' she continued.

Nick knew what she meant, Cammie too. The plan was for them to return home for a week, then once the album was mastered, play three U.K shows. A trial run, of sorts. Then a year of touring in Europe, America, South America, UK by Christmas..

'I don't know, Dom…' Nick felt light headed at the thought, a cymbal shimmer of anxiety down his spine. He needed more tablets. Scotch? Meditation? He wasn't sure if much would help with *the fear*.

The Big Man's PR guru Pesos had secured them five lucrative shows in Europe, headlining a string of festivals.

They all had a second helping of gruel. Nick and Dom went out for a cigarette on the Veranda, making sure to pop the coffee machine on beforehand. They agreed on real Irish coffee, followed by studio until lunch, the studio until nighttimes.

'Ok Nick, let's take it from the top. Dom, you come in on the 4th kick drum..'

It was eight P.M. The trio were feeling weary but Cammie had just recently sourced his stash to aid them along. The silver tray reared its presence once again. Nick took a swig of Estrella and waited for Cammie's pre-recorded drum part.

'One, Two. A one – two-THREE FOUR!' screamed Nick.

The drums came in strong, Nick grated his Fender Tele, ripping at the strings, pummelling out the chords. Dom bobbed her head, as if on stage, and Cammie was moving in his lair, they could see. Cammie had decided on a pick me up for them all, followed by the addition of some strobe lights amid the usual altering colours. Nick was trying some screaming for the first time, Dom noticing he had a remarkably Cobain-esque voice now. This was the last song they'd decided on, and it was a slight departure from their other songs, but they all loved it. They'd all been big grunge fans growing up, Cammie especially, Dom and Nick veering into Brit-pop as they got slightly older, thanks to elder brothers mainly.

Nick wanted to try and get the energy of it all onto tape, spending hours recording different feedbacks and guitar effects. He'd even played Cammie some Nine Black Alps, to give him a general idea. The song itself, titled 'Dawn Drain', was catchy though. It had a hard posterior, mangled guitars and wailing, but at its core it was a pop song, whatever that was.

'That's fantastic,' Cammie had remarked as they went for a playback in the adjoining room. 'Sounds like The Kinks getting the shit beat out of them...'

It was this comment that was to be stuck in Nick's head for days. And also why he was desperately hoping Cammie would consider joining the band. He'd even noticed Cammie and Dom had many similarities, and wondered if they perhaps liked one another. Nick was always the last to notice these things. Ana asked him out initialy. He didn't even know she'd liked him, he just remembered they'd gotten along really well after they'd met.

The recording process had taken a slight detour by 10 p.m, and maybe it was their combined inebriation, but they decided to go and listen to some music in the sitting room. They opened another champagne, with the crate that had been left looking a bit lonesome now. Never mind, there was another in the Outhouse. Dom played The Slits, Cammie let them hear an upcoming rapper he was due to produce in two weeks, and Nick worked his way through some alt. Indie classics, starting with Pavement and The Shins. It had turned into another party, of sorts.

'I had an idea this afternoon.' Dom had laid out lots of ingredients on the bunker. Cacao, icing, flour, sugar. 'I'm going to make Joanne a huge cake that she can share with the locals. As a thank you.'

Nick and Cammie agreed it was a great plan, and helped weighing out measurements and beating eggs. The three somehow found themselves covered in flour, a mini food fight erupting. Nick inhaled a line. Had a sip of champagne. Flung a spoon of cake mix into the air, it hitting Cammie square on the head. Dom erupted, and ran over to tickle him. He was squeamish, and grabbed an egg, cracking it over Dom's head now. 'You bastard!' she cried, the three of them in stitches.

The song finished and they stood momentarily, 'Luckily the cake's in the oven by now.'

Dom was removing the shell from her hair, laughing, with Nick puffing cocoa dust out of his shirt.

'Hey, guys do you mind if I talk to you a minute?' said Cammie.

'Yeah sure,' replied Nick, taking a seat on a barstool in the kitchen.

'I've been thinking, you know, about what you said. With the band and everything…' Nick and Dom glanced at each other, they hadn't expected this.

'I've been working for years. I've been around. I'm 31 next

month. I've been lucky, but all I've really seen is my equipment, you know. I love it, but I've always been envious of the people around me. I love the new material so much. It'd be an honour going on tour with you guys. I want to experience more from life, from now on. See the world, appreciate experiences.'

Dom got up and gave Cammie a huge hug.

'That'd be ace Cammie!'

Cammie cracked a broad smile, the music starting up again.

'Absolutely,' said Nick, giving him a handshake now. 'You'd be perfect for the band, Cammie. You're so talented.'

'I just can't wait to play live, and see different places with you guys. I'm really going to make the most out of everything from now on,' he went on. 'I've got this rap album to produce in New York, and then we're mixing in London,' he pointed at Dom and Nick. 'And I'm free after that.'

'It's great news Cammie,' said Dom, changing her top in the kitchen.

'But also,' he continued, 'I've noticed my lifestyle taking its toll on me. Mentally and physically. Nick, I know you've gotten some help too. Do you think we could do the touring without any… stuff?'

Nick and Dom hadn't expected this either.

'Well, yeah. I mean…'

Dom was actually glad at Cammie's suggestion. She'd even considered saying it to Nick herself, months ago.

'Absolutely,' said Nick. 'I also want to. I've been thinking the same recently. I've done so much and sometimes I can't remember half of it. I don't want to… take things for granted anymore.' Nick stroked his chin. 'It'd be good to remember things, never lose my sense of wonder.' Nick thought a minute.

'That'd be a good song title actually.'

The oven pinged just as if just on queue.

'Take the cake for a good example,' said Dom, removing a loaf-sized chocolate cake from the oven. It looked impressive.

'Are you OK with that? Seriously?' asked Cammie, cause it would have to be. 'I've been doing this like…'

'Honestly, Cammie,' Nick went on. 'No more drugs when we meet in London. Not for me anyway.'

The three had made a mutual pact. Something they all wanted to change, but always had an excuse not to.

'Don't get me wrong,' said Nick. 'I like getting high. But I always will…'

They all knew what Nick meant.

'It'll take a big change. Effort.' Added Dom.

Cammie felt he may have brought the tone down a little, but was relieved to open up to them, his new bandmates after all. They were a threesome now. A band of brothers.

'Pass me that sweeping brush,' shouted Dom.

Nick slid on The Beatles '1' album, a band favourite. Nick could see Cammie's phone flashing. He passed it to him, surprised he was getting reception.

'Hey,' he said.

'Hi. Is it a Mr. Cameron? I'm Ana. I am the partner of Nick. I've been trying to call the three mobiles. We're at Edinburgh Airport. I've been calling…'

The line was weak, breaking up.

'Hello? Oh Ana, like from Mr Fazio?'

'Yes,' a female voice replied.

Cammie understood who it was. Nick and Dom exchanged a glance. The phone line went dead. Cammie moved towards the other side of the room, trying to get reception. 'Shit,' he said, looking at Nick and Dom. 'It was Ana. Something about Edinburgh Airport. They're there,' he said, 'I think.'

The three of them were taken aback. They hadn't expected them until Monday. It was Saturday. Nick grabbed his phone from the teak table, but couldn't get through. Dom then tried too.

'I'll go out and try,' said Nick.

'Don't bother,' said Cammie. 'I think they're coming. Seriously man.'

'Oh shit,' laughed Dom.

Firstly, they were all still high. Very high. A slightly sweaty and clammy high.

'OK. Let's think about this.' Nick was pacing around the sitting room.

'We've got to clean up, for a start,' said Dom, making her way to the cleaning cupboard.

'To the Batcupboard!' shouted Cammie, opening the cleaning cupboard at the back of the kitchen.

He grabbed a Henry hoover, and started waltzing around with it on, multi tasking to 'She Loves You' on the stereo.

'Nick, open the door, let the smoke out.' Ana was spraying the kitchen, panicking, scooshing pink lather all over the place, laughing at Cammie.

'With a love like that /
    You know you should be
    Glaa-aaadd.'

They both sang in tandem now. Nick took a fall over a guitar peddle, cake mix sploshing over his skinny jeans.

'Bahahah,' cried Cammie, still hoovering.

Even Dom was laughing now.

'You're a sick man. I'm getting my shades,' said Nick, making his way to his feet.

He gave Cammie a middle finger and grabbed a black bag. Empty cans, ashtrays and food stuffs were rammed inside. Dom was cleaning the surfaces, the sink.

Cammie was doing his best with Henry. Nick was on a mission.

'It's got to look like how we found it,' reminded Nick, and they both agreed.

They continued cleaning.

'What about the rest of the house?' inquired Dom.

'Well, luckily we've only used our three rooms, and the pool,' shouted Nick, now at the far end of the living areas. 'I read in my e-mails Mr Fazio has his own quarters, on the other side, so it's All right. Don't panic man.'

Dom was now mopping around the marble buttock art instillation in the corner. The place was looking a lot better already. Presentable, even. A pop went off, causing them fright. It turned out to be Cammie, having sourced the champagne crate from the outhouse. He'd decided to open one.

'Bottoms up!' he shouted. Dom laughed, polishing a right buttock.

'Indeed Cammie.'

The three stood scratching their heads, an air of anxiety and mischief in the air.

9

A loud, galloping whir could be heard now. Louder, and louder. It was an intense crescendo of whapping, like the flock of a hundred buzz-saws. A horrible white light bathed the sitting room. All three approached the patio doors. A helicopter was hovering in front of the house, slowly descending toward the front grass. Its engines were loud, not to mention the propellers. A heat could be felt from the machinery, a whiff of acrid petroleum now. A white shirted man landed the machine. A small airbus, perhaps. Big enough to fit maybe six people, Nick considered.

'Whoa. That's pretty awesome,' said Dom.

The machine looked otherworldly; the three had earlier been excited by a trice passing the Batmobil, exceeding its 15mph. The three stood and stared, like rabbits in the headlights. Almost literally, were they to spot one. Suddenly, the engines cut off. With the side door unbolting, sliding. It revealed Ana, The Big Man, and two other men unbuckling their seatbelts. The band all stared at one another, nervous. Hearts pulsating.

The men were out first. Then Ana was lifted out, with the Big Man taking the steps. His jet-black shoes looked expensive, plonking down the steps one at a time.

Ana was first over to the group, hugging Nick and Dom instantly. She looked radiant in a red dress, her long black curls full of life. Cammie shook her hand. Mr Fazio was approaching, sharply dressed in a suit as always. Nick also recognized one of the men as his security and driver from Barcelona. The other he didn't know. Mr Fazio shook their hands one by one, then walked toward the patio doors, now opened by one of the two men. The other walked alongside him.

'So...' he said.

He flicked some dust particles off his shoulder. One of the men had returned to the helicopter, unloading bags and suitcases with the pilot now.

'So, so, so...'

The Big Man took a breath and stared around the room. Ana stood with the others, cheerfully. Nick hoped his eyes weren't like Dom or Cammie's. Two Cents apiece, so they were. He'd forgotten to get his shades. Mr Fazio addressed the two men in Spanish, raising an arm to the far end of the house, giving directions, Nick assumed.

'I tried to call,' said Ana to the three.

'Don't worry,' said Nick, looking back at Mr Fazio.

The Big Man was quite tall, considered Cammie, who had only met him once, in Hamburg.

'So do you like the house?' asked Mr Fazio.

They all nodded. Cammie at the back chewing chewing gum.

'Absolutely sir,' he said. 'Nice to meet you.' He moved forward and extended his hand.

'Papi, this is Mr Cameron. Ingeniero De Sondido,' said Ana. Mr Fazio glanced at him.

'Yes, we've met once. In Germany, no?'

Cammie had put his hand down.' 'Ah. Yes. I do remember the place. It was Casimero's' Party.'

'Yes yes,' said Mr Fazio, smiling at Cammie. 'You came highly recommended. From New York. And, tell me. Have they been behaving?' he nodded his head toward Nick and Dom.

Nick wondered if he was joking, but felt like he was a lined up at school somehow. 'Yeah, of course sir,' said Cammie.

Dom felt herself trying not to laugh.

'Good. I hope you've enjoyed your stay.' Mr Fazio smiled at them all, easing the room up a little. 'I'm hungry. Anyone for dinner? One hour. Sigueme' He turned around and walked across the sitting room.

The two men followed, both wearing the same colour of suit. The three men exited the area.

'Shhh, I hope the pool is clean,' said Cammie, making a juvenile quip Nick and Dom hoped no-one had heard.

Ana was hugging Nick again. 'So great to see you all!' she said, always full of energy.

'You too,' said Dom, polishing off her glass.

'Champagne,' announced Ana. 'Great! Let's get more Dom. The helicopter was a bit bumpy. How have you been?'

Dom and Ana got on very well, so much so Nick would often resort to reading a magazine when they got together.

'And Cammie. Come over.'

Ana had the same unintentional command her uncle had, Nick had picked up on it recently. She was being friendly but often gave orders without even noticing. Nick found it quite cute. She carried herself in a certain manner.

'So you're from New York? I've never been. Tell me about it.'

Nick and Dom took the opportunity to tidy up the last crumbs of debris left in the kitchen, admiring the cake on the bunker. Cammie was deep in conversation, as they'd expected. Nick just beamed when Ana was around; Dom had noticed it from the first time they all met in Barcelona. It made her happy. She really liked Ana, and they always chatted over vegetarian recipes and clothes.

One of the two men entered and addressed Anna mid conversation. They exchanged phrases.

'Ah. OK.' 'Who would not like to eat meat, with dinner?'

'Just us I think.'

'Solo Dos,' replied Ana with a smile.

The man walked to the kitchen and began looking around, checking all the cupboards for ingredients.

'Hello,' he said to Nick.

Nick felt uncomfortable and in the way, so joined the others on the couch. He'd been waiting for a pause to talk to Ana, but the conversation was moving swiftly, changing.

'Tell me about your album,' enquired Ana, who had been a big fan of the band before they'd even been introduced. 'The big question: Is it as good as the first?'

'I think it's better,' said Cammie. 'But don't tell Nick.'

They all laughed. A pan was sizzling in the kitchen now, the man was obviously a keen cook. Nick had always loved that about Ana, she was amazing in the kitchen. Her parents owned their own restaurant in Barcelona, not a pretentious place, a little bistro that served the most delicious authentic dishes.

'He is making some el pescado, seafoods, potato croquettes, and vegetarian paella. Some other things.'

They chatted about music, the house, the far Isle, and soon the smell of herbs filled the house. The second man had set the table, and was conversing with the cook. They both had unusually big shoulders, Nick noted. Handy with a knife.

'Anyone for a cigarette before dinner?' asked Dom.

'I think Cammie got lost in the restroom,' laughed Ana.

Nick and Dom laughed too, perhaps not on the same wavelength. Perhaps so.

Cammie joined them outside eventually, having changed into a more formal dark green shirt. Nick and Dom weren't too fussed. Mr Fazio had seen them drenched in sweat, kicking their amplifiers on stage. They could see Mr Fazio in the sitting room now, on a lone armchair, listening to 'Daytripper'. He looked more relaxed. Ana went inside, they began conversing in Catalan.

'I didn't expect a helicopter!' whispered Dom.

'I'm buzzing guys,' said Cammie. 'If you go into my room, there's two Himalayas on my bed side table.'

'Jesus' said Dom, making a cutting motion at her neck, whilst marching inside.

Dom and Cammie found it amusing, especially when Nick went upstairs.

'Come on, better go in.'

The man who had prepared the delicious food had put four bottles of Granache on the table. Corked and chilled. They all got seated after Dom came in, having changed her top, of course. Mr Fazio took the table end, Nick and Ana followed; then Dom and Cammie. The men brought out dishes, placing them all long the table.

'Some tapas to start,' said Ana. She ran through them all, letting Dom know which ones were vegetarian.

'Now,' said the voice, from the top of the table. 'Can we just...'

Mr Fazio and Ana bowed their heads, closing their eyes. Nick followed. Then Dom and Cammie. They realised they were saying grace. They sat in silence for ten, twenty seconds perhaps, before Mr Fazio raised his head.

'Enjoy.'

Nick couldn't help but snigger at Dom and Cammie, trying their best to be sensible. He hoped they hadn't lost their appetites. Mr Fazio was dishing himself some squid, chatting to Ana in Catalan. His suit was very fine, a very dark grey, tailored with glimmering cufflinks. He'd put his napkin around his neck, which he'd always done in Barcelona. The two men didn't join them to eat, and stayed in the kitchen making small talk.

'So Ana tells me you've had a nice stay Nick?'

'Yes. Indeed. And thanks again.' Nick always tried to make an effort recently. He had felt a bit guilty about owing Mr. Fazio money, and courting his niece.

'Thanks too,' said Dom.

'How's the barn studio? Is it OK? I hope you've made some music.'

Nick tried to consolidate the question, knowing Mr Fazio was perhaps hoping for news of an album. A return, pronto.

'Yes. Luckily we've used it a lot, sir. We've recorded a full album now I think,' he glanced at Cammie, hoping for some back-up.

'Yeah it's state of the art, sir. I had some stuff brought from New York. But it sure is a great Studio to work in. The aerodynamics of the space. The audio interface bridges the…'

'And, how are you Dominica?' Mr Fazio cut Cammie off mid-sentence.

Dom crunched on a broccoli stem.

'I'm erm, well, sir. Having a great time thanks.' Dom was always fairly relaxed around Mr Fazio, and she didn't seem too alarmed by what he said. She'd once even remarked to Ana that her Uncle looked like a sinister Pavarotti, which had left Ana aghast.

'Good.' He returned to his meal, looking serious once again. He began conversing with Ana again, in Catalan.

Ana looked at the three, nodding. 'Yes, I told my uncle you've recorded ten songs already.'

They all nodded.

'That's good news,' he said. He placed his napkin on the table. 'The fish is very fresh, no?'

They all nodded.

Ana poured Mr Fazio more wine, ushering the others to do the same.

'May I ask how you are, sir?' Nick asked.

He wanted everyone to ease up a little. He hoped after a few wines Mr Fazio would too. He seemed stern tonight.

'I'm well. I've been in Chile. I met Ana in Barcelona. We had a lunch and then came to Scotland. I try to rest when I come here.'

Nick nodded.

'I like to surround myself with good people in life.'

Nick caught Mr Fazio's eye, he made Nick uncomfortable, staring into his eyes. Nick and Dom were accustomed to these remarks, or terms Mr Fazio often used. They often left them both baffled, or biting their lips.

'You're in good company, sir,' shouted Cammie up the table.

Mr. Fazio smiled at them all, reserving a raised eye brow for Cammie.

The plates were cleared away, with more dished promptly being served. The food was delicious. Cammie gave a thumbs up to the chef, though wasn't sure what exactly their role was.

'You'll need to let me hear your music. Perhaps tomorrow.'
They all nodded.

'You know. Where I grew up, in a village, we used to fight over who got to play the music. Start the dance.' Mr Fazio said, pausing. 'And nowadays…kids still queue up to buy vinyl. It never changed.'

They all agreed, nodding. Dom and Cammie whispered to themselves briefly.

'Yeah, if it's trashy euro-pop…' muttered Cammie.

Dom gave him a swift elbow to the rib.

'Hey Dominica.' Mr Fazio went on. They were all enjoying the risotto. 'How many vegans does it take to change a lightbulb?'

Dom rolled her eyes, she smiled, unconvincingly.

'Yes, Mr Fazio?'

'Papi..' said Ana, cringing slightly.

'None. They can't change a single thing.'

Cammie burst out laughing, followed by Nick. They were both somewhat drunk, but the uptight atmosphere seemed to make it even worse. Cammie was nigh-on bent over.

'Oh god,' said Dom.

'Ok, Papi. No more jokes please.'

The men went around the table, filling up the Grenache. Their expressions were humorless, vacant. Nick thought of a conversation starter now, but was a little stumped. 'So we got to meet some of the local people down at the pub,' announced Dom.'Very kind.'

They began chatting about the Isle. Ana had never been to Scotland before, she told them, inquisitive about the locals.

One of the men approached Mr Fazio, who took a telephone to him.

'Excuse me,' he said, not looking too thrilled at the interruption.

They were telling Ana about Mr Finn's guitar playing, his time in New York in the 70s. About Bob Dylan. She was transfixed. Mr Fazio seemed to be deep in conversation in his native tongue.

'No. No no no. Nine Thousand. Yes Holiday. Interummpes Mi Cena!' he screamed down the phone, banging his fist on the table.

Wine glasses shook. He handed the telephone back to the man, who scuttled off, and seemed to finish the conversation for him. His face was ruby, his teeth clenched under his jet-black goatee. He rubbed at his neck tie. Silence. Ana coughed, smiled at them all. The awkwardness was palpable.

'Anyone care for Crème Caramel?' said Mr. Fazio, calmly.

They all nodded. Champagne was poured, served. Mr Fazio took out a small Cigar, admiring it as it smoked in the ashtray. 'Strawberry Fields' didn't seem to be the perfect background music somehow, Nick thought to himself.

'You know I saw Paul McCartney once. Madrid.'

'Cool,' said Dom and Cammie.

'I was thirteen. My cousin and I had got three tickets, somehow. We sold the third ticket for twice the asking. So we bought a thousand cheap cigarettes from a market vendor. Sold them all at the concert to hippies, trash you know. All floating around in Sgt. Peppers outfits. The next day we both bought a suit, went to a matinee. Ate dinner. Good times.'

Mr Fazio smiled and took a huge puff of his cigar. He blew

smoke all over the table. He pushed it aside and nodded to his aides. Nick and Dom always got aggravated at his description of certain music fans. It's not as though Fazio had exactly brought much to the musical table. The men brought out dessert, which looked dazzling.

'So tomorrow we meet and I will hear the music.' Mr Fazio hadn't so much asked a question as told them his plan.

He and Ana began conversing in Spanish briefly. She whispered to Nick, assuring him they could spend lots of time together. Dessert, coffee and biscuits were enjoyed, laced with chats about the Spanish Royal family, Antoni Gaudi and Guillermo Dell Toro, who the band were all fans of. Mr Fazio joined in on occasion, but hadn't looked too enthused. He finished puffing on his cigar and rose to say goodnight.

'Enjoy the house,' he said lastly, 'I'll see you tomorrow at six.' He waived a hand at Dom and Nick, who returned smiles and thank yous.

'Que Descanses Papi,' said Ana.

One of the men followed, whilst the other began clearing the table.

'It was nice to meet your Uncle, Ana,' said Cammie eventually.

'Yes. But I know he's tired,' was Ana's response.

They continued their night listening to music, with Ana and Dom becoming engrossed in their own chat regarding Spanish fashions, where Nick and Cammie in home recording techniques. Nick and Ana said goodnight around midnight, and left Cammie and Dom to watching Summer Of Soul, munching popcorn.

'Dom and Cammie are getting along well,' said Ana, having

noticed a chemistry early on in their company.

'Yeah,' said Nick. 'I'm glad because,' he paused. 'I think Cammie is going to join the band too.'

'Really?' said Ana, unaware of his even playing the drums.

'Yeah, he's a fantastic drummer, and writer too.' Ana seemed impressed. 'That's great news Nick, after everything, you know...'

Nick knew what she was referring to.

'Hey, when did your Uncle get a chopper? What was that?'

Ana laughed a little. 'It appeared in Edinburgh, he must have hired it or something,' she waived her hands. 'He doesn't like boats, I think...'

Nick showed Ana their room, and they were deep in chat about the album, her parents, her new part-time job in the city at a publishing house. Nick loved spending time with Ana, hearing all her news.

He sometimes found it hard to believe Ana's father was The Big Man's brother. Her father was a small but chatty man. The family owned a Spanish café and bakery near Barcelona, in a bustling city community where Ana grew up. Ana would spend most of her time there, making coffees and chatting to customers. It wasn't too far from their flat either. Ana's father had always used humor to address any big issues, whereas Mr Fazio now seemed to be the polar opposite.

'Is everything OK with your uncle?' asked Nick now, having noticed a slight intensity about him at dinner.

'Yes, I think so. It's family stuff, you know.'

Nick thought to change the subject, so told Ana about the local pub, Cammie's Golf buggie, and their typical daily routine.

The main thing was she was finally there. They had all agreed to have breakfast around nine, however Ana had unpacking to do, and Cammie was already arranging his return to New York in a week, to record a rising rapper from Baltimore.

10

'Ey Up Nikolai,' said Dom in the kitchen to Nick, who was making two lattes, having sunk his usual morning mug of espresso. 'Sleep well?' she chuckled, nudging his rib, making him snigger.

'Yes Dominica. And you? May I add...' he winked at Dom. She was a little taken aback.

'Shut up Nick,' she said. 'I was gonna show Ana the Lighthouse this afternoon,' added Nick.'

'Cool, but remember we've to be back at six for the Big Man,' replied Dom, in a hushed tone.

'All right, see you later then. Hey hold on Dom... Aren't you making two coffees?' said Nick, making his way upstairs with a cheesy grin.

Touché.

Back at the room Ana was engrossed in a novel, she always read in her spare time, and had turned Nick onto lots of Spanish writers. He was overjoyed when she had got the job with the publishers, and thought it to be her ideal venture, other than becoming a chef.

'Anyone good?' Nick inquired.

'Yeah. It's for work, actually. They've asked me to proof-read it, give them feedback.' Ana replied.

'That's great. They must be impressed with you Ana.'

'Well... I don't know,' said Ana coyly.

Nick put down the coffees and suggested the pair go out soon.

'What can we do?' asked Ana.

'I've got a plan.'

Cammie had returned to the barn studio to continue working on their album with Dom, who'd wanted to fine-tune her recordings some more. Nick noticed Mr Fazio wasn't around, assuming the men were staying on the other side of the house.

'Papi will be around later,' said Ana, who was making breakfast for them. Nick loved Ana's cooking, and she was always excited to visit new places and try the foods.

'I'm not sure what you'd make of a lorne roll with brown sauce,' said Nick.

'A what?' asked Ana, serving up warm churros with Scottish lavender honey she'd picked up at the airport.

'That's amazing,' said Nick, saving some for Dom and Cammie for later.

The two went outside shortly after for a walk, but Nick had a plan. He had borrowed Cammie's key last night for the Batmobil, so hopped on and started the engine.

'You can't drive!' laughed Ana, slightly puzzled at the now-flag-covered contraption.

'Hop on, I'll take you on a tour.'

The pair skidded down the path, giggling and listening to mostly Ana's latest Spanish indie recommendations. Though Nick could understand some of the lyrics, he always found himself concentrating on other parts of the songs, picking up on guitar riffs or unusual structures.

'There's the pub,' pointed Nick, skidding round a bend by the entrance. 'Mr Finn's house is just up here.'

The Batmobil had taken on an odd kind of burping noise at the chassis, but it still moved. They gave a wave to Flavio at the allotment, whose heavily tattooed body was catching some rays. He must have been daydreaming with his sheath-in-hand, for he didn't return the gesture. He spat on the ground and followed the golf cart with his eyes. Ana liked to study people, and was overcome with a sense of Dé Jà Vu, but with the man. She'd only experienced this a handful of times in her life. He looked back, menacing and aggravated, to say the least, and had made an odd sign with one of his hands. He'd thrown the sheath onto the muddy ground. Nick thought he may be slightly mentally afflicted, or impaired. His fingers were crossed and he made an O shape with his thumb and index fingers. He held it toward them, like some kind of gang sign. Nick shuddered a little, odd behaviour on a sunny day in the Country.

'Nick,' said Anna loudly, as the Batmobil spluttered away from the allotment. Guitars wailed on the Batstereo.

'Who was that man there? How did he know this sign? It's Spanish code.'

'Who Flavio? It's what? He's a farm guy at the allotment. Anyway look up here, there's an orchard.'

Ana was silent a few minutes, Nick evading potholes and enjoying the music at 15MPH. The Batmobil had been through the wars, All right.

They drove on; the mist had cleared to unveil a sunny afternoon by now. Nick had promised Ana he'd take her to try Joanne's fish and chips sometime, and she was asking about the locals, possible professions on the Island. They drove on and eventually got to the Lighthouse. Ana couldn't help but feel a little uneasy about the man at the allotment, but didn't want to spoil a nice afternoon. Things were on her mind now.

Her lifetime of anxieties seemed to follow her around like an invasive plague.

Nick pulled up the buggy by the bench, and unveiled his pre-made picnic, made up of champagne, olives, cake, hummus, breads and cheeses. 'Quite the chef,' said Ana, surprised.

Nick had even brought two glasses and plates, and they sat on the bench taking in the scenery. The sun bright and the tranquility was bliss, unusual for them both. No zooming cars, no rubbish, no queues.

'Ana, I had hoped to talk to you.'

'Yeah? What's the matter?' Ana was a little confused momentarily.

'I've had a lot of time to think since I've been here Ana. Reflect on the past two years. On us.'

Nick was fumbling in his pocket now, taking a deep breath, looking a bit flustered. He went on. His words had to be perfectly placed. His mouth was like a cactus pot.

'Ana. I've missed you. I realise you mean everything to me. I wanted to ask you something.'

He produced a box, which he had gotten in Barcelona at Ana's favourite jewelers shop before leaving.

'Would you like to be my wife?'

He opened the box, producing an elegant silver ring the jeweler had kindly helped him choose. Its shine radiated from the sun. Her mouth was slightly agape and Nick found her to be genuinely surprised.

'Of course, Nick! I'd love to!' She took the ring and gave Nick a lasting kiss; luckily it had slid onto her finger perfectly.

Nick embraced her for as long as he could, she had pulled away to dry an eye, clear her throat. The pair were so content and relaxed, they sat on the bench for hours, chatting and laughing, sharing their favourite memories since they had met.

They laughed over the one time Nick had shown up for a date, his arm in a sling from a radio gig in the afternoon. Nick reminisced about Ana, turning up to a book signing and producing a rival author's book by mistake, having left in a hurry. She retorted with the tale of Nick being chased by a swan in his skinny jeans, running along Spanish lake after feeding it chips. They finished up the champagne and sat awhile more, before realising they'd have to be back at the barn soon. They stopped off for a pint of Guinness at Ana's request, which she seemed to love, comparing it to coffee. Joanne had gotten along with her great, and she was excited to hear all their news.

'We'll be back for fish and chips,' promised Nick, upon their departure.

Back at the house the pair found Cammie and Dom in the Bolthole, who had spruced the place up a bit and removed the usual shrapnel of debauchery. They told them the news, and they were all overjoyed, though not too surprised, Nick had mentioned it to Dom a few times previously, though hadn't had the opportunity. Ana had made a brief departure to go and phone her Mum, with Nick hoping Mr Fazio would also be pleased. Cammie had made him nervous by playing the Jaws theme tune on a keyboard when he mentioned it.

'Quit it,' joked Nick.

Just at that the door opened, unannounced. A man, one of the two, entered the room. Mr Fazio followed; he walked slowly toward Nick in his deep burgundy suit and extended his hand. Nick looked up, and shook his hand, relieved and anxious in equal measure. Mr Fazio sat down on a stool by the mixing desk.

'I've made coffee for us all. We brought some cakes from my favourite Deli in Barca. I'll see you in the sitting room in ten minutes. Bring the CD.' Mr Fazio waived his hand at Dom and Cammie, so as to say hello.

'Great,' said Nick. 'We'll be right up.'

Mr Fazio left the room, and three conferred he must have had a busy morning.

They met in the sitting room, the table covered with cakes, churros and bunuelos. Champagne had been opened, and coffees made.

'A toast,' said Mr Fazio now, Ana hanging on to Nick, her nose snuggling his neck. 'Thank you Mr. Fazio. And we all wanted to say thank you for your hospitality and…'

Dom and Cammie nodded in agreement, glad Mr Fazio appeared to be in slightly better spirits today.

'Now.' He took a sip of his champagne. 'I've got to leave tomorrow,' he announced. 'Things in Barcelona. But do join me for dinner. Ana is staying for a while, and I will see you.' Mr Fazio took another drink of his champagne, looked at the glass. He looked at them all, taking off his shades. 'Now,' he said, making his way across the sitting room. 'Let's enjoy the snacks. Mr Cammie, could you provide the musica?'

Cammie moved towards Mr Fazio with the CD in his hand, goofily crunching on a warm churro.

'These rule,' he added. Mr Fazio had lit another cigar.

'I've not heard it either,' whispered Ana now, remembering she was yet to hear their work.

She reminded herself she was going to hear one of her favourite bands' new albums before anyone else. They all took seats around the couches and enjoyed the assorted finger foods and drinks. Cammie turned the volume up a little, not too loud but enough to impress, he'd hoped.

'I hear you are also quite the drummer?' said Mr Fazio, turning to Cammie now.

'Yes sir. I've been playing for years. Nick and Dom's new material is...'

'Well. Just don't charge them as much as you do me for recording.' Mr Fazio found this hilarious, an elongated wheeze as he puffed cigar smoke around the room.

Cammie had too, momentarily. Now he looked a little put out. The CD began playing, Nick and Dom were relieved.

'I hope it's not all B-sides, now,' joked Mr Fazio.

'Papi, stop it!', ushered Ana.

His two aides seemed to laugh at his jokes too. Nick and Dom were a little nervous. The album played, with peppers of conversation taking place throughout. Ana was excited to hear Dom sing. Cammie explained he'd only worked with a few bands, as opposed to artists, previously. They discussed the track listing. Overall Ana found it to be better than their debut, but was eager to hear it again. Mr Fazio hadn't made any comment on the music thus far, but was tapping his feet occasionally and remarked on the strength of the vocal harmonies, nodding to Dom.

The album finished and they all sat for a while, hoping Mr Fazio would be pleased. There was silence. More silence.

'I like it. I think you have done very well. I think you will return my investments...' Nick and Dom seldom heard any comments from the Big Man regarding their music, even after chaotic shows, so took this as a good sign.

'And you too Mr Cammie. Good work.'

He got up having finished his second glass of champagne, and they all arranged to meet for dinner in the dining room at nine o'clock, after Mr Fazio's swim. The band and Ana decided to deliver Joanne her cake, and sauntered down to 'our local' as Cammie had got to calling it. They found the phrase amusing in his NY accent. They were all relieved at Mr Fazio's comment, though succinct. He'd liked the album. Ana was thrilled, playing it whenever possible now.

'We've got a present for you Mrs. Joanne' said Cammie as they all entered the pub.

It was quiet, being a Monday night. It seemed to be open every day.

'It's a chocolate cake.' continued Dom.

'To say thank you.'

Joanne seemed to love the gift, and was surprised they'd made it themselves.

'So very thoughtful,' she opined.

She got her digital camera from somewhere. 'Let's get a picture of you all,' she added. 'I promised Eilidh, my daughter.

And also, I want one for behind the bar!'

The four of them all posed, Joanne joining them for a final snap, with even Dino the Dog getting in on the action. 'Awww,' said Ana, patting his head. Joanne loved to show off her Shepard. They left him chomping on an old fishing net, by the door.

They headed back up to the house for dinner, on foot for a change, to let the Batmobil rest. Cammie had taken a couple of beer mats to stick to the exterior. They all got seated around the table, the smell of a rich basil sauce filling the air. Mr Fazio was yet to join them, but he'd be with them soon. Cammie wanted to know about Ana's favourite Spanish writers, merging into a chat about Barca's best cinemas, somehow. They'd all agreed on a game of Monopoly later, and Cammie promised to make them all his famed smoothies the next morning.

The second of Mr Fazio's aides was around now, mingling and assisting with the cooking. The bigger of the two seemed either to be at Mr Fazio's side or constantly on the phone. Nick and the others had assumed he knew little or no English. Nick had attempted to start a conversation with them already, whilst in the hallway, but hadn't had much luck. He thought one of them had called him a 'mook' behind his back, but wasn't completely sure. Mr Fazio had entered now, having had a swim, and was enquiring about dinner. The chef had made delicious looking pot of beef stew, and a vegetarian casserole pot for Ana and Dom. A large basket of fresh bread and was laid out, along with a selection of meats, olives and vine tomatoes. Mr Fazio insisted on champagne and wine this evening, followed by grace. Mr Fazio made polite dinner chat, joining in where felt to add anything. Cammie took his chance to speak.

'Seeing as it's your last night Mr. Fazio. Could I ask you any good stories, or your opinion of the Music industry?'

Mr Fazio sat for a while, and then took off his glasses, and placed them on the table, beside his plate.

'You know,' he began. 'All these kids are the same.' Mr Fazio waived his arm at the room, as though describing ants. 'They come to me in their latest fashions, wining about heartbreak. They want to be famous. T.V. But once you know the ins-and-outs of the music business, it's no different to any business.' He paused for a second. 'Do you think I don't have to pay to have a potential summer smash played on daytime radio? I do. So you've got Mr DJ. A greasy parasite. He wants X. So I deliver X. X gets publicity, at a cost, then Y and Z gobble it up. In the process making them dance when they're drunk on an 18-30s holiday.' He bit down on a piece of beef, patting his mouth, now. 'Then hopefully they buy it. Or maybe for their child.' They were all listening, trying to take it all in. Like following steps. 'I'm just lucky they have no taste. Or the IQ of let's say, a flaming, used toilet roll. But recently, Cameron, I can afford to deliver something with quality. Like IKEA did, eventually.'

Nick almost spat out his hors d'oeuvre.

'The point is. I can create gold from toilet paper. Or from a folded napkin. Viola. Speaking of which, anyone care for desert?'

Nick wasn't sure at where to start, but thought better to not. He understood Mr Fazio's point, it's just that it also raised more questions. His brain was like a pinball machine.

'The bottom line is, embrace the post-moronism,' said Fazio in a bored tone.

'The what?' asked Dom. 'Is that a thing?'

'No. I made it up.'

They all exchanged glances. Nick was sure Mr. Fazio had compared his music to a napkin. Meaning it was better than a pile of flaming toilet paper, or something. And a bit about IKEA? Mr Fazio's analogies were becoming ever the more eccentric, he was sure. He liked the phrase 'post moronism', however. He could probably work with that. One of the men had put on some smooth R+B, so at least some Muzak.

'OK. Well enough about all of this. Do you like erotic cinemas? I am thinking of a new 3D venture.. It has dollar bills written all over it...'

They sat in silence, other than adding a solitary, 'Interesting.'

Cammie was trying not to laugh. Everyone was still rather puzzled, deciphering Mr Fazio's philosophy. The desert had arrived, and luckily Fazio was keen to eat up his black cherry sorbet, rather than continue talking. He gulped down an espresso. He looked uninterested. He lit up a cigar and sat back. He fiddled with his goatee a bit. 'And you wanted a story, Mr Cameron? Here's a good one. There was an artist I wanted to sign. A greasy little mook called Diego Dolla. A Cuban hunk, set-to-be pop sensation. He wanted money. Big money. Twice as much as I offered him. So, he went to my rival record company. Then in the end... I let him go.'

They all looked, surprised.

'You let him go, sir?' asked Cammie, confused.

'Yes.' He paused. 'I had my men dangle him upside down,

naked, above the city square. Then I threatened to let him go. He signed our record contract the same evening.' Mr Fazio stretched his arms out, and had a puff of his cigar. A few giggles and laughs could be heard.

Was he joking? Thought the band, the table. His men hadn't laughed.

'Time for a rest.' He placed his glasses back on. Completely solemn faced. 'I will see you all again, soon. Congratulations Nick, Ana. Enjoy your time here.'

Mr Fazio placed a hand on Ana's for a few seconds. He got up and left, slowly. They all sat with mouths slightly agape. The Big Man strikes again.

'Who wants coffee?' said Ana, smiling awkwardly. 'They have lovely Italian over here.'

11

'OK guys, well, it's the homeward stretch.'

It was approaching noon, and Cammie had arranged a meeting of sorts, on the Veranda. Perhaps it was Mr. Fazio's fables, or a sudden urge to get organised.

'We've got most of the album recorded. Mr. Fazio seems quite impressed. We'll be mastering in London. Then it's all systems go, I guess... The promo run, touring, sightseeing.'

The band was having a small meeting after breakfast, on the patio. They'd been awoken by the helicopter at nine A.M, Mr Fazio and his aides ducking into the shuttle and zooming toward the mainland. Ana had gone to see him briefly beforehand. Nick however, was luckily otherwise engaged in biting his fingernails.

'Yep. There's still a few final things I want to do regarding the recording Cammie,' said Dom, and Nick agreed, now onto his second mug of tar de espresso.

'I think we've made great headway. I'm more proud of this record than anything I've done.'

Nick seemed somewhat content for once. No one had particularly minded the Big Man's presence, and they were grateful for his hospitality, however there was a relaxed air around the place again. Certainly less intense.

'You guys.' Cammie had something he wanted to share with them, for he looked a little ill at ease.

Nick wondered if he had perhaps had a session to himself last night.

'I was just; It's none of my business. But. Erm…' he was scratching his head now. 'In New York, you know, I've come across a lot of people.'

'Are you OK, Cammie?' asked Dom, sniggering to one side.

'What it is, and I may be wrong, But Mr Fazio seems to be a little… Unsafe, you know. Maybe? I mean, y'all think he might be dangerous?'

The two of them laughed out loud.

'Cammie are you paranoid?' said Nick.

'How much of that Colombian did you take last night?' jibed Dom.

'Oi, give me some while you're at it.'

Cammie looked a little relieved, but still, something in his behaviour was a miss. 'So I'll take your word for it, then. That's cool. I just don't wanna be involved with some shady cats, you know?'

'It's fine, Cammie,' said Nick. 'He does own the label. But I think you're - we're - safe. We're not going to be hung from an ivory tower, if that's what you mean.'

'Have a beer. Relax,' said Dom. 'Why don't I make us some lunch and we can get together to work this afternoon?'

Dom headed into the kitchen, rummaging around the meats and pantry items that had been left.

'This could feed a small army,' she concluded.

Following a delicious mushroom and chive frittata thanks to Dom and Ana, Nick and Ana made their way to the bedroom, for some time alone. Ana had wanted to talk to Nick, she too seeming a little thoughtful today.

'Are you OK, Ana?' he asked, as they made their way down the hall.

He slid on some Modest Mouse and got a seat by the window in their suite. He kicked off his loafers and did a few stretches, inspecting the book Ana's work had given her. 'Any good?' asked Nick, however Ana didn't reply.

'Nick. I've been thinking now. I need to talk to you.'

Nick didn't like Ana's tone and felt a severe ping of anxiety rush through him.

He knew Ana, and knew when they were headed for a serious chat. He crossed his legs.

'What's up Ana? Did I do something wrong?' Nick thought he had executed his engagement plan perfectly yesterday, and began to wonder what was up.

'No Nick. It's not you. I'm so happy we are engaged, but I've been losing sleep last night. If we are going to be together there's some things I will need you to understand.'

Nick was puzzled, himself becoming a little paranoid now. What could it be?

'Is it the band?' he pleaded.

'No Nick. Just listen.' She went over to Nick now. 'So you know I have a big family, and my family is very important to me.'

'Yes. I'm glad they are Ana. It's only normal to…'

'Nick, please just listen to me.' She interrupted, seeming slightly irked.

Nick stared at her, and wondered what could have upset such a beautiful creature. Her black long hair, elongated curls slinking over a pure white dress.

'If we are to be engaged, you'll have to listen…'

'My family are a big family Nick, and sometimes we have to work to support each other. I didn't choose this life, but it's what I've been brought into.'

Nick wondered what she was talking about. Were they criminals? Gypsies? Aliens?

'My uncle is a powerful man, Nick. He is a main head of the Latosra Catrel. He is, we are, I suppose, a Mafia family.' She paused.

Nick paused.

'There. I've said it.'

She sat back down on a chair, facing him. Nick sat for a long while, a crescendo of questions stirring inside now.

'Firstly Ana, are you taking the piss?' said Nick, leaning forward.

'Nick I can assure you I am not. I cannot agree to marry you unless you know who I am. My father is no longer involved, but my uncle answers only to a Mr. Pinto in Chile. We are Latosra. We are, what some might call, the Spanish Mafia.'

Nick couldn't believe what he was hearing. He almost felt to laugh, as though it was part of a reality TV show. Punkd, perhaps. But Ana looked deadly serious.

'Ana. So you're telling me The Big Man…sorry Mr Fazio, your uncle, is a leader in the Spanish Mafia?'

'Correct,' said Ana, again slowly taking a seat next to him. She took his hand, felt its coldness.

'Please don't use the word Mafia, I don't like it. The recording company is a smokescreen, Nick. He is very wealthy, yes. He needs smaller businesses to invest in and control. It's complicated. But I am trying to distance myself from it all. It's dangerous.'

'Dangerous? Aye, you're no jokin,' said Nick. 'I'm due him money, Ana. The Band are... I'll wake up in a garbage truck.'

Nick was puzzled, slightly angry now. He had mounting thoughts around everything.

'Ana, I need time to process this. I'm sorry. It's not your fault. But... What?'

Nick needed a cigarette.

'Nick, I love you. Go and have a breather. I knew you would take time to understand..' Ana still seemed a bit upset herself.

'I love you too, Ana. Of course I do... but I need some air, I'm sorry.'

Nick made his way downstairs, he could smell chlorine. The others must be doing their lengths, he thought. Where's that pool guy?. He poured himself a large glass of single malt sat on the bunker, and went outside. Pacing now, back and forth behind a cigarette. The more he pondered the situation, the more it seemed to make sense. The cafés. His numerous houses. The black cars. Suits. The 'aides'. They were henchmen, probably, he thought. Peru. Mr. Fazio in general. Everything made sense. He remembered back to the time Ana and he had been welcomed for dinner in Barcelona, and one of the waiters had started shouting at the Big Man, and been marched out of the building promptly. Nick and Ana assumed he was drunk. Or the time The Big Man had gotten an ovation at one very nice café in the City, Dom and Nick had been a bit confused, but thought he might be a part owner. Ana had told Nick he was en entrepreneur, due to his running of the music label and a large string of cafés and a cinema in the City. He even knew the city Mayor.

'Nick,' Ana came outside now. 'I don't want this to affect us. Our relationship.'

Nick lit another cigarette. He stopped and took in his scotch. It burned ruthlessly. He rubbed his chin.

'Me neither Ana. I just can't believe it, you know? And your dad, is he involved?' 'No Nick. Not any longer. He was happy to run the café and my mother insisted she wanted nothing to do with it. My father tries to keep a distance, you understand?'

'So are you protected?' urged Nick, slightly panicked.

'Yes Nick. I don't expect you to fully understand. But you will in time. Please keep this to yourself, OK.' Ana made her way back inside, closing the patio doors.

'Fucking hell.' Nick blew a massive puff of smoke out. He unfolded a wrap from his inside jacket pocket and sniffed it harshly, caking his nose in dust. 'Where's Cammie?' he thought to himself.

'Hey Nick. How's it going? You look occupied.'

It was Dom, eating a banana by the door, now.

'Starting a bit early today. Are you celebrating the Big Man's departure?'

Nick had jumped a little. He wasn't expecting anyone.

'Just leave it Dom, eh?'

'All right, All right.' Dom knew not to press the issue, she could tell by Nick's demeanour instantly when something was wrong.

He clammed up like a tortoise. A swift change of the subject usually did the trick. 'Have you had your meds today, Nick? Hey… you know I was thinking, we should do something fun today? It's supposed to be twenty nine degrees after midday. Also, it seems getting to the mainland is a lot safer now, by the way. Monica the PR was on the phone earlier. The tour is going ahead.'

Nick sighed. He could sense Dom's efforts at lightening the mood.

'Sorry,' he said. 'Well, that's good. I've just got to see Ana and then I'll come and see use. Have a think if we can do something fun, then. But I'm not going bloody cockle pickin' in my neon trunks.'

They both smiled a little.

'I've put the coffee on. I'll see you in a bit, Nick.'

Dom headed inside and left Nick, assuming he was skulking about something or the other. Probably the space between tracks on the album, or something. Nick took the chance to go and see Ana. He had lots of questions, but figured in time things would become cleared up. He was glad at her honesty, the situation just held such weight. Not exactly like disliking the in-law's cooking, or their choice of pet name. Ana was in the suite, catching up on her book, taking notes here and there.

'Are you OK?,' she had raised her head. She looked a little sad.

'Yeah I'm OK. Thanks for being honest. I guess it's just something we'll have to work around. I mean, are you involved in all of this? What's your position, so to speak?'

'Nick... it's fine. My parents have kept a distance from it all, where possible. I don't know what'll happen in the future. I try not to think about it too much.'

She got back to her reading. There was a knock on the door. Nick could hear Dom and Cammie, chortling in the hallway.

'What's up?' asked Cammie.

'We were thinking of taking the Batmobil up to the diving

ponds Joanne told us about. 'There's some cliff jumps,' he said. 'Scary but fun.'

Nick considered throwing himself off a cliff, a fitting idea for the day. 'Cliff what? Ponds? Aye.' He rubbed his chin.

'Cammie's done great work on my songs by the way. Trumpets, everything. Oh. We've got life jackets. They were in the garage. Along with a nice selection of Vermouths.'

'All right. Count me in. Ana, you want to jump off some cliffs into the sea today?' Nick turned his head back to them, still in the hallway.

'She's in. See you downstairs.'

The four piled into the Batmobil, Dom's choice of James Brown 'Singles Collection' a fitting backdrop to the midday sun. Cammie had kept the map Joanne had drawn for them, wavering it was just up the coast from Mr Finn's House. Nick wondered what they looked like, driving along in the Batmobil at 15mph, all wearing lifejackets and shades, listening to J.B and sharing slugs of Vermouth.

'This is a great adventure,' said Cammie, his collection of flags and trinkets growing ever vaster on the Batmobil.

'Yeah it is,' agreed Ana. 'Scotland is so tranquil, you know?'

'It's not all like this. Try playing a gig in a Kilmarnock pub car park,' laughed Nick.

'Did you get paid in Irn Bru?' asked Cammie.

'For gods sake Cammie. Watch the sheep!' cried Dom. They bobbled down up and down along the coast, past Mr. Finn's house, 'Superbad' erupting in a miniature sing-along. They waved at Sailor Jerry, a local whisky drinker at the pub, off to work. 'Hey you know I was thinking about Mr. Fazio this morning. He's an interesting man.' said Cammie.

'Yup,' added Nick, feeling a cold tingle down his spine.

'His story reminded me of my boy Amos. A guy I had recorded in Houston, a rapper.' They were all listening now. It's a good Industry story, you know. My boy had finished his album, which was pretty good. Perfect production-wise of course.' continued Cammie.

Dom laughed.

'So his people had sent out promo CD's to all the right sources. Radio stations, hip-hop magazines. Promoters etc. Then I'm reading Hip Hop Houston one day, and I came across an article. It had called his album 'Houston Heresy'. They trashed it. Two stars out of five. So I called him up. Told him. He wasn't happy…'

'And,' asked Nick. 'Then what?'

'My boy knew who had written it. He'd always thought they were cool, you know. He'd kissed his ass at a party, in fact. So my boy approached his girl one day, rolling in a fresh Maserati. Hired of course, but never mind. Anyway, he managed to get the reviewer's number. Sent him a selfie of him on the beach, eating ice cream with his girl. On the teacups at the promenade.'

They all laughed, shaking their heads.

'The teacups? Aye Cammie. It's cut-throat business out there,' said Nick.

'I'm sure that went down well,' added Dom. 'Indeed'.

Ana didn't say much, she'd been fairly quiet all morning.

'Hey, we're nearly there. Up to the left,' said Dom, a pencilled piece of A4 flapping in the wind.

'Let's go surfin,"' said Cammie.

They decanted a picnic of Vermouth and pre-made sandwiches, fruit and meats. Towels, the music, beers, even some sun-lotion. They all walked along the coast until they spotted the pools. One, two, three plunge pools. Bright green in colour, almost lucid, but clearly deep.

'Wow,' said Cammie. 'Shit's like Avatar or something.' They all stood and stared at the pools, took photos. A breathtaking sight, completely untouched, picture perfect. 'Ok, I'm going into the small one first,' said Ana. Nick felt a relief, realising he was now probably responsible for her safety more than ever. He didn't want to end up in a waste disposal truck.

'I'll go first,' said Nick.

He leapt, unannounced, into the pool. The three exchanged glances. He had gone under briefly, now his head bobbed up above the water.

'Phew,' said Dom.

'Joanna said they was all safe, should be cool,' added Cammie.

He got hold of Dom and Ana's hands on either side, and on three, they jumped. Twenty feet perhaps zipped past in two seconds and boom, they hit the water. They began splashing around, and could hear 'Try Me' playing from up above. Nick scooshed a mouthful of water at Cammie, realising how strong the salt was now, couching harshly. It was refreshing; the freezing water sent instant waves of electricity all over your body. They managed a few lengths, the pool being the size of a large room, and made their way back up the rocks. Cammie had gone below to check the depths of the other pools, deciding a decrepit long stick might work.

'Whoa. That was a rush,' added Nick, picking seaweed from his arm.

'I might even try the third one. After lunch. Don't want to die on an empty stomach.' Dom and Ana hadn't found his joke too amusing, Dom straining the salt from her purple patched fringe. They got seated and sunbathed a while, sharing stories and shots of vermouth, which Cammie had taken a liking to, comparing it to wine with sour candies.

'I'm sure it's a bit more complex, Cammie' Ana had teased him.

They could feel the sun beating down, the salt acting as natural frying oil to their skin. It was nonetheless, utter uninterrupted relaxation for a couple of hours. Ana wanted to play them an experimental band from Barcelona, which somehow ended in Cammie going on a tangent about Mogwai's guitar sound.

'All right. So whose going to brave the Big Dipper?' said Dom, getting to her feet, wiping the salts from her skin. 'I'm roasting,' she added.

They had all got up now, teetering towards the cliff edge at the third pool. It was vertigo inducing.

'That's around thirty five feet I would guess.'

Nick wasn't too keen on the experiment. Although the pool at the bottom was vast, it didn't feel entirely safe.

'Joanne said she'd done it. In her thirties,' added Dom. 'It's real deep ya'll. I checked it out before. I'm doing it for sure.'

This was Cammie now. He took around five steps back from the ridge and said 'Watch me!' in his best James Brown impression.

'I'm Superbad.' He ran off, a slight jump at the end. His body simply disappeared. The three exchanged glances, surprised.

'Cammie!' Ana had approached the end now, they'd heard a boom. Cammie's head was bobbing, floating.

'It's awesome,' he shouted, criss-crossing his arms. 'I guess it's safe.'

'I'm scared', shrieked Ana as they all prepared for the plunge. They took steps back, leaving a run-up of around ten feet.

'OK,' said Nick.

He took their hands on either side. Dom had her eyes shut, ever so slightly. They crunched down on his hands.

'Let's goooo…'

They all began to run, jumping at matching heights, their hands coming unstuck mid air. Nick felt his stomach moving up toward his throat, and managed to take in a view, sideways for around a second. It was beautiful. He rushed through the air, suddenly slapping the water and plunging below. The icy sensation was crippling, almost. Like a shock to every cell in your body. It reminded him of a dream he often had before flying, for some reason. Falling endlessly before he'd wake with a CLAP, usually sweating. His head burst up through the cool water. He took a huge breath, again tasting the strength of the salt instantly. Ana was ok, laughing with Dom. Nick wrung out his hair in the water, floating now. Cammie was on the rocks, finding the whole thing hilarious.

'Whoao,' said Nick. 'That was unlike anything, man. My body's buzzing. Let's do it again!'

Following repeated jumps, flops and thanks to Cammie's efforts, an eventual dive-bomb from the cliff, they decided to call it a day, and would stop by the local on the way back to the barn. It was becoming a tradition of sorts, an outing usually ending in a round of Guinness and wines. They told Joanne about the pool dive, and she was surprised they'd done it more than once.

'My husband tried to tell me not to. So of course I had to,' she laughed. 'Oh. I sent my daughter the photo of us,' she added. 'She loved it. She can't wait to buy your next album.' She smiled.

'Well, tell her it's almost finished,' said Nick. 'But it's a departure. It's Calypso House,' he said, donning a straight face. 'Nah I'm only joking Joanne. More of me whining, I'm afraid.'

Joanne didn't seem to know how to reply, so thought best to fill the Guinness as Nick said hello to Dino the Dog.

Nick and Ana agreed to share tea making duties, so back at the barn Ana prepped some veggies for a spicy casserole they could all share, while Nick opted for a poached pear and ice cream desert.

'It's amazing how much I could attune to the simple life,' pondered Nick.

'You said it was like fucking Springwatch' shouted Dom across the sitting room. 'No traffic, clear air, pleasant people. It's just, different, hey.'

They all agreed, feeling the benefits of the day's cold water therapies.

'There are pros and cons though,' said Cammie, now. 'The lack of new culture and small things like shopping, eating out. It'd probably get to you after a while. I'd be taking vacations to Milan and Miami. It's all relative, I guess. But yeah, it's been real nice for us. Plus I got good skin for once too.'

Dom and Cammie were relaxing, watching a Scandi-Noir chiller, chatting about Dom's brief trip to Norway once. Nick took the opportunity to squeeze up to Ana in the kitchen, chopping courgettes.

'We've had a great day. Let's just try and enjoy ourselves and maybe can have a catch up later?'

'Yeah, I've had a fun day too. I don't know what to tell you. I've just been honest and open. You know me.'

'I have concerns, of course I do. I have questions. But I'll chat with you later, OK?' They squeezed one another's hand and had a cuddle, a mouth-watering mix of spices and pesto dancing the air.

'Dinner's up, guys…' called Nick, opening another of the eighteen or so Grenache's that had been left.

Ana gave nick a nudge and rolled her eyes toward Dom and Cammie with a smile. They were chitchatting away on the couch, close, like an old married couple.

12

There was a commotion in the house. Nick heard a 'Boom' on the front door. Panic. Boom. Boom. He rose up, smacking his knee on the bedside table, grappling to get his jeans on. Panic. Boom. Boom.

'Ana. There's someone at the door. Ana!' Nick gave her arm a shake.

She was in a deep sleep. 06.55 a.m, read the alarm. Nick didn't need the light, he realised the sun was up, so made his way down the hall. He stopped at the staircase hoping to get a good glance through the glass door. Figure out who it could be. He saw a fuzzy, yellow neon outline.

'Coming,' he marched on.

Boom. Boom.

'Aye, I'm here! Fucki…'

Nick opened the door a jar, expecting to see Cammie drunk, or perhaps Dom had crashed the Batmobil. Who knew. He opened the door swiftly, causing it to shake. It was the police. Panic.

'Good morning, sir,' said the man on the left, sombre of tone and fully clad in constabulary get up. A man in a suit stood next to him.

'Hi there. I'm Sergeant Millard, and this is Inspector Gunn from the Scottish Police Department. We were hoping for a moment of your time.'

Nick rubbed his eyes, bare-chested and bed-headed. He could feel prickles on his skin, burned but chilly from yesterday's diving.

'Yeah, of course. Sorry. Aye, aye come in.'

He noticed two police vehicles and an unmarked Saab in the driveway. He knew this wasn't a routine neighborhood chat. The policeman entered first, glancing around the space. He didn't seem to be in any great rush. The suited man followed, his lip pursed over a grey moustache. He looked stern and completely emotionless.

'Thank you. Now, then. We were hoping to ask if an Ana Fazio is currently staying at this address?' said the PC.

Nick was panicked now, racking his brains as to what could be going on.

'Yes. Yeah she does. Ana, she's my partner. Sorry. Fiancé. But can I ask why? What's the problem?'

The inspector stepped forward now.

'We were hoping to have a chat with you all, particularly Ms Fazio. Perhaps you could get her for us. It's regarding some unfortunate news, I'm afraid. Take your time, sir.'

'Yes. Aye of course. I'll be back in two minutes.'

Nick frog hopped up the stairs, noticing Dom and Cammie's lights were both on now. He headed straight for the suite to get Ana. Ana had woken and was sitting on the bed, dazed in a crop top.

'What's going on Nick? Is it an emergency?'

'No Ana. I dunno. It's the police. They're downstairs. There's about six outside. This is lookin' serious.'

Nick paced around the room a little, whilst Ana went to the bathroom for a few minutes. His leg hurt from bashing it on the dresser. Ana hadn't spoken, a yawn seeming to suffice. Nick grabbed a polo shirt from the cupboard, remembering he had some items he wouldn't want to be found.

Ana came from the toilet and Nick ran in, 'Need a pee. Sorry.'

They got ready to see the officers. Nick was out after disposing of the last of his treats. He didn't know where else to put it. Would they come in? His nostrils burned like two chilli peppers as he stuffed a rolled twenty into his jeans. Oh shit, he thought. This should be fun. He grabbed his phone and tried to ring Cammie. No reply. Ana had taken his hand now and was leading him down the hall. They made their way downstairs to see the officers standing in the sitting area. Ana squeezed Nick's hand. His heart began pounding. Racing thoughts, racing thoughts.

'Hello. Ms Ana Fazio?' asked the PC.

'Yes…' she replied, timidly. 'How can I help?'

'Would you like a coffee?' asked Nick. 'I'm having one.' He popped on the machine and returned to Ana promptly.

'No, thank you. Is it OK if we have a seat, perhaps?'

'Yes aye, yes come in.'

They all got seated in the sitting room. Nick's palms were sticky. Ana looked worried. 'I'm afraid I have some bad news for you ,Ms. Fazio…' explained the PC.

The inspector sat placidly, turning a button on his sleeve. He stared at them both continuously, however. Ana caught Nick's eye briefly, she looked concerned.

'I'm afraid there's been a helicopter crash. Just off the coast, towards the mainland. Yesterday morning. We have a crew and all air accident personnel working at the scene. However, I'm sorry, but there were no survivors Ms. Fazio. We believe your uncle was on board, as were two of his associates.'

'No. No. Papi? No no.' Ana held on to Nick's shoulder.

'How?' Her head went down. 'Nooooo…' She was sobbing suddenly.

'We're sorry Ms. Fazio. We're doing all that we can to examine the evidence and wreckage.' The two officers sat in silence. Ana wiped her eyes now, sleepy and puffy. 'I'm so sorry Ana,' said Nick, consoling her as best he could.

He was shocked too. He was lost for words, a little stunned.

'We'll give you some time to gather your thoughts. However we'd like to speak to you all individually in say, half an hour. We'll come back.'

The two men got up from heir seats and headed for the door. Nick and Ana stayed seated.

'Can I help, sir?' asked Nick, unsure of what to say.

'No, Mr. Black. We'll be back shortly. We're aware this is a difficult time.'

Nick moved in to Ana again, hugging and rubbing her arm.

'Ana. It's All right. I'm here,' he whispered.

Ana was quiet. Nick could feel her deep breath on his neck. He was glad the officers had left them in peace.

'This is so awful,' sobbed Ana.

Dom and Cammie had heard most of the conversation, and thought it best to tip toe back to their rooms, whispering along the hall. They had both heard about the crash from the stairwell, and been equally as stunned as Nick. After Ana had managed to gather herself, Nick made them coffees. Nothing much was said, they were merely slightly puzzled about the officers returning. Anna's sobbing was receding now. Nick made his way to the bathroom to phone Cammie, but was met with an answer phone. 'Bloody signal,' he thought. He popped a bit of chewing gum in his mouth, flushed the toilet.

'Ana, I'm just going to wake the others OK? I'll be back in two minutes. I'll need to tell them to be dressed.'

Ana had turned the TV on for some background noise, music, anything. She stared blankly at the box, and gave little response. She hoped it had been an accident. Anything else seemed unconceivable. Her Papi was gone. She began to weep again.

Dom entered and gave Ana a huge hug, consoling her when possible. Nick and Cammie followed, their heads bowed down. The front door went again, the bang a mere polite knock this time. The officers entered again. Not two, but three, four, five, six, seven. The PC and moustachioed detective stood at the front. 'Now, we don't mean to alarm you. But we would like you all to step out with two officers per person, for routine questioning. You do understand this is a routine precaution to gather information. Ms Fazio if you would like to join Inspector Dwight at the front, Nick Black please join the officers to your left. They were all led into different rooms, areas. Nick didn't see where the others were going. Before he knew it he was sat in a drawing room on his own, clutching his mug of espresso. His palms were sweating now. Truth be told, he was buzzing.

'Where's Ana?' he inquired.

'Please don't worry sir. We need to talk to you all individually. Just a few questions.' The officers sat facing him now. Both expressionless, bar the odd rub of the chin, pout of a lip.

'So, shall we begin?'

'Aye,' said Nick, a shrug of one shoulder.

He crossed his legs. He chewed his gum. He hoped his dilated eyes were undetectable.

'Yes, let's begin sir. Now on the night of Mr. Fazio's leaving the property, may I ask you what you did, sir, and whom with?'

'Sure. We'd been out, at the pub. I remember we'd made a cake for the landlady, sorry- for Joanne. So we decided to take the cake down to the pub. It's the only pub. Anyway. So we did that, stayed for a few drinks. Nothing fancy. Then we left and came here. Me, Ana, Dom and Cammie. And in the house would have been Mr. Fazio and his two friends. Associates. People.'

Nick was confused, but considered it was just routine questioning. He hoped he could see Ana soon.

'So do you recall seeing anyone out of character, at the pub or returning to the house at all?'

The moustachioed man now. Twiddling away on his 'tache like a Highland Poirot, thought Nick. He stifled a laugh.

'Nope. I'm afraid not. It was all local men, who were known to each other. Then me, Ana, and the other people I've mentioned. We came here, and didn't see anyone. We had food. Mr Fazio went to bed fairly early. We stayed up until, one am or so. That was it.'

'Thank you Mr Black,' said Poirot.

He seemed happy enough. He held a dictaphone of some sort in his hand. He pouted his lips very far out. He sniffed.

'Now, you said you are engaged to Ms. Fazio. May I ask how long you have known her uncle? Are you aware he owns this property?' said the PC now.

They were doing a tag team, thought Nick. Like two wrestlers. He'd seen the good cop bad cop scenario on TV, and hoped neither would turn out the latter.

'Yes I am. To cut a long story short, he offered us- the band, to come here to record our second album. His artists occasionally use the place to record. It has a studio and all that

131

stuff. He owns a record company, who distribute in Europe. Anyway, Ana and I have been together for over a year, and we met through Mr. Fazio.'

Nick couldn't think of anything else he could add. He took a good slug of his coffee. Strong. He shrugged his shoulders and let out a big sigh.

'It's really bad all this, you know...'

'Yes Mr Black, we understand. Just a few more questions.'

The detective slid his glasses back up his beak and sat back. The PC smelled of Lynx Africa.

'Mr Fazio was a wealthy man. He had connections in various parts of Spain, South America, Europe in fact. Has Miss Fazio ever discussed Mr. Fazio's other working roles in these areas Mr Black? Were you aware of this?'

'No. I'm just aware he is, sorry, was, my Boss, so to speak. He owns our record label in Europe, so I have met him on numerous occasions. I didn't know any of the other men here either. They couldn't speak English.'

Both of the officers sighed at varying times. They sat in silence a while. One officer, Millard, went to speak. He changed his mind, as if thinking. And sat back again.

'OK Mr Black. If I was to ask you a simple question, may I ask now?'

Nick was on the verge of perspiration by now. His heart was beating. It's the coffee he thought. The coffee. Chew your gum Nick. Racing thoughts.

'Yes. Ask away officer.' Nick smiled.

'Were you ever aware Mr. Fazio may be involved in any criminal activity, at all?' 'No, I was not,' replied Nick. Be astute he thought. 'No I was not sir.'

'Very well,' said Gunn now.

Clicking his pen. Tapping it on the table. The questions went on. They wanted to know more about Mr. Fazio. Any conversations Nick had had with him that may have seemed unusual. How long he had known Ana. Had she ever spoken to him about her uncle? They even mentioned Ana's dad, the friendly café owner who'd always made Nick feel welcome, given him dynamite-strength coffees.

'I think that should be almost all,' finished Gunn, eventually. 'Now lastly, can you think back very hard?' He paused. 'Was there ever anyone at all inside this house, when you were here, other than anyone we have discussed already?'

Nick sat for a while. Twenty seconds, perhaps. Was it a trick question?

'No. No there was not. Cammie had people here before we arrived. He's our sound engineer. They were his men, team. No that's it. Me. Ana, Joanna, Dom, the Finns- oh that's right, Mr Finn and his wife, they live on the island. We invited them for dinner, we met through Joanne. That was it. That's all.'

Nick shrugged his shoulders and raised his arms.

'Yeah. We've been self-sufficient, pretty much. Eating, watching movies, recording, sleeping, cleaning. That's it.'

Nick sat back. He couldn't see where this was leading, but understood their questions. 'Yes that's all. Can I ask why you're...'

Nick felt a sudden jolt of memory. A green jumpsuit. The pool man. 'The guy at the pool. Of course.' A shiver went up his spine. He had paused mid sentence.

'Hold on. I did see another person. In the pool. Cleaning the pool, while we were recording once. And then again a few days later. He was here, but I didn't ever pay any notice. I was pre occupied. But I saw him twice...'

The officers were suddenly all ears now, clicking pens sitting forward.

'I see,' said Millard, a stray lip pointing upward. 'Another male, did you say? Did you ever speak to the man? Can you remember anything about him?'

'Yeah. I saw him once while we were recording. A green jump suit, grey hair, quite thin, between fifty and sixty I would guess. I was kind of busy, you know. I had no reason to think anything of it.' Both men were scribbling now. Taking notes it seemed.

'And the second time please?'

'I came down a couple of nights later to get a glass of water, and I saw him in the garden, kind of hanging around I guess. I looked at him, and he looked right at me. He kept his stare. It had freaked me out a bit, to be honest. He smiled at me in a funny way. I just went back to bed, thought he was a bit odd though.'

'Can you remember any particular features about the man?'

'No sir. Not particularly. Just middle aged, white-ish hair, looked a bit like Christopher Walken. The actor guy.'

Nick felt perplexed. How could he not have remembered? The odd man who had been around, had given him a eerie smile once too, through the window at night. He'd felt a bit scared but he hadn't thought anything of it, but then, why would he?

'Why is this important officers, are we not safe or... Is something going on?'

Nick was becoming slightly worried now. Ana had told him about herself completely now, but surely there was nothing sinister going on? The men stared at Nick, blankly. PC Gunn finished jotting on his pad and rubbed his chin.

'OK I'll tell you where we are, Nick. It would seem from the evidence we've gathered thus far from the helicopter, we're having it analyzed. It seems there may have been some evidence of, of foul play, so to speak.'

'Foul play?' asked Nick.

'What, like a crash? Like a bomb or something?'

He took a minute to gather his thoughts. He wished he could speak to them like friends, not in this strange situation. Truth be told, he was also inwardly buzzing. His decision to get rid of his drugs in a paranoid state was causing him some strange sensations. He hoped the officers hadn't noticed too.

'Thank you for your time, Nick,' continued Gunn. 'We will of course be seeing you again, and rest assured all the correct measures are being taken at this time. We will be leaving a police vehicle, manned, outside, until the investigation is over.'

'OK…' said Nick, unsure of what to say.

He was running through scenarios in his head. Had the big man been gotten rid of? What was he involved in? Where was Ana?

'Thanks officers. If I can help just let me know. Do you know where my fiancé is?' The officers took a minute.

'Yes Mr Black, she may be slightly longer in questioning, but rest assured you'll see her soon.'

The two men got up, gathering their papers and dictaphones. An investigation? He finished up his coffee. Deary me. He followed the men to the sitting area. His jaw was clenching up. Palms feeling a bit greasy. He just wanted to play some music.

'Thank you officers. I'll see you out.' 'Thank you Mr. Black, that won't be necessary.' They left the house and got into the black Saab on the driveway. Nick could smell Lynx in the air.

'I didn't tell them anything. What could I say?'

Dom was having a peppermint tea with Cammie and Nick. Nine thirty two am now. It'd been a minor rollercoaster already. 'Me too. Shit's crazy. They said there was something with the chopper...' Cammie generally felt the same way. They hadn't seen the pool man Nick had spoken of and he'd never mentioned him. He'd have assumed he was a caretaker or cleaner. But the house was never cleaned.

'As far as I know it was only ever us,' added Dom.

They all sighed, their thoughts zipping in different ways. Dom felt a bit panicked by the thought of a random man prowling around whilst they were there. They were saddened about Mr. Fazio and confused about the situation overall. Ana was nowhere to be found. A police car sat in the driveway, still and unused. Two officers were reading iBooks.

'Nick, remember that time I spoke to you on the tour bus?' went Dom, 'About what Sophia had said?'

Nick did remember, and it made all the more sense now. But he wasn't about to tell them what he knew. Not now.

'Yeah I remember vaguely, Dom,' replied Nick, not looking too interested. 'She told me to be careful of Mr. Fazio. And never to disrespect him to his face. He was connected, according to her.' That was a bit weird...'

Nick simply nodded, as he had at the time. Sophia worked for their record company in Barcelona, and helped with the band's photography occasionally. She'd pulled Dom aside, or whispered in her ear once after a photo session. Cammie didn't say much at all. He felt largely unconnected to the whole thing, to Mr. Fazio. He was paying him handsomely to record an album; that was all he knew. He ran a label. Had made a lot of money. It was nothing new to Cammie. In fact compared to some of the rappers he'd come across, with teeth more expensive than his NY flat, Mr Fazio was pretty regular.

'Hopefully Ana will be about soon,' said Nick. 'I'm just going to chill upstairs. Listen to some records or whatever. Bye.'

They all parted ways, Cammie heading back to the Bolthole, Dom to catch up with family and check the band e-mails. There was a fair bit to think about, and Dom didn't want to mention anything of it to Mr. Fazio's associates or record people, who she was becoming a lot less trusting of for some reason.

Nick waited in the suite, had a shave, put on some records, quietly. He wasn't sure what else to do. He skimmed through Ana's book, but couldn't read it, it being in Spanish. He paced around a little to some Strokes b-sides. He smoked a cigarette out of the window. He was bored. Bored yet buzzing. Really buzzing. His heart was going like a propeller. He opened a beer, thinking it might calm the nerves a little. Where was Ana? He was keen to see her, speak to her. Kiss her. He didn't want to ponder on the situation, it held too much weight, and caused him anxiety. He took some of his tablets. He paced some more. The Cribs now, one of his favourites. He paced some more. His telecaster was sat in the corner. He poured over its striking dark green colour. He remembered nearly breaking it after climbing a speaker stack on stage once. All the places it had been. All the places he'd been. Still in one piece. And now he was here, on a remote island drinking beer at eleven A.M, avoiding talking to PC Poirot about the Mob. Crikey.

He got up, and decided to get changed and join Cammie in the Bolthole. He had some new song ideas, wanted the band to practice and be ready for the tour. Cammie was already immersed in his usual position, behind his laptop perfecting the recordings. Probably mastering a tom tom sound, or something to that effect.

'Hey Cammie. I had to get rid of my stuff this morning. I'm buzzing. I didn't know what else to do.'

'Oh shit,' said Cammie, swiftly removing his headphones.

'I forgot too man. Do you think I need to? Shit I got quite a lot in here...'

Nick shrugged his shoulders.

'Aye, I would if I was you.'

Cammie raked around a little, producing a small, mini-egg shaped ball.

'Shit. I had one of my guys bring this in with the equipment, from New York.'

He rubbed his chin, stretched out his arms.

'I can't throw it away Nick. Shit man...'

Dom entered the room now, she wanted to pop in with some coffees, see what was going on with the recordings. Cammie explained his predicament.

'Can't you hide it?' she suggested.

'Nah,' said Cammie. 'I can't afford to get caught. No way. I gotta finish it today.' Cammie opened the bag and poured it all out onto his trusty tray. 'I was gonna quit anyway.' He used a ruler to chop it out. 'Three each first' he added. 'But don't hang around.'

Cammie took two in succession. He held his nose, the blood rushing to his head.

'Jesus Cammie!' went Dom. 'Take it easy.'

Dom had even peeked round the door, she too was having pangs of anxiety. Nick and Dom did the same, Dom almost choking in the process. Cammie again. The same. They all sat back. They were all breathing heavily. Cammie had a brain-wave, and put on the album, from track one. He wanted them all to experience it together. As a band.

Slowly, it raised and raised, the opening track was possibly the best, an instantly uplifting gem Nick was stoked to have written. His body was pumping. Dom was smiling. Cammie was bopping his head. They were mutually tingling as one. The drums kicked in, like horses galloping into battle. The bass-line now, swerving around, fluid. The tambourine claps, the feedback. It was as perfect as it could ever sound. The three held hands and listened to the song in full. Nobody spoke. There was nothing you could add or take away to make it better. Timeless. Cammie had managed to splice the two opening tracks into a segment almost, using feedback and echo, touches of Nick's vocal. It had a more mid-tempo feel, acoustic guitar and strings but with a great melody. Cammie had always said it had a sad side to it, an unexplainable melancholy most great pop songs tap into. They'd all discussed it a few times, with everyone from ABBA to Beach Boys coming up. They all seemed to know what it was. It took on a greater effect in the current situation, and they all sat in silence, buzzing but letting the emotion flow over them. They continued, listening to the album in full, Nick hoping someone would come with news about Ana, or where she was. He wasn't overly keen on seeing anyone in his current state, but dearly wanted to see Ana.

They all agreed track eight was definitely an album highlight, which pleased them all. 'Listen to any good record, if track eight ain't great, it's a coaster man.' This was Cammie's way of describing any records he deemed not a classic. They could be well used to plop your coffee cup on. Nick and Dom took it as a compliment. Next was the second of Dom's tracks, Nick noticing how much bolder it sounded now. It sat on the record perfectly, and her vocals were incredible. Nick was amazed she hadn't had the confidence to sing entire songs yet, as opposed to great harmonies. The album was nearing the end, with the heaviest guitar-wise left for last. It definitely had a punchy, Nirvana feel to it. Not grunge but not punk. Something slightly different. They'd all agreed it would be a strong way to close the album, shards of flailing feedback, drums falling apart and bottles breaking. You could almost hear the Bolthole being trashed by the band. A chaotic, paranoid grimace.

There was a sudden tap on the door. They all exchanged glances. Could it be Ana? She'd been away for hours. Three, four, perhaps. The door opened a jar and Ana was outside. She hadn't come in, looking sad but also worn-out. Nick got up and went outside immediately.

'How did it go? Was it OK?' he asked, trying not to seem too worried.

'Hey. Yeah, it was OK. I'm just going upstairs. The police are away but the car must be staying outside.'

Nick walked Ana to their suite, and was conscious not to ask too many questions. She didn't need any more of that, he was sure. 'Let's just go and relax,' he said. They went to their room, and Ana lay on the couch. She was quiet. Nick thought to go and make coffees, and thought of possibly suggesting a film she'd like to watch. He made the lattes and returned to their suite, Ana still staring blankly at the room. They agreed on a TV series to binge on, though none of them were particularly fussed. Ana was quiet gathering her thoughts. Nick was quiet, his mind like a pin ball machine, but quiet. He finally told Ana about the man he'd seen. About how he hoped it wasn't at all, in any way connected. He was paranoid enough as it was. And he knew Ana had grieving to do. They pondered over various scenarios, but it was looking ever more like Mr. Fazio had been snuffed out. They stayed there all day, processing the recent events.

13

'I will have to go back to Barcelona early. I need to speak to mama and papa today.' Ana was on the bed, contemplating getting up, facing the world.

Nick was shaving, glad the whole event as over. He felt refreshed having binged on Walter Presents dramas and Nordic Murder Mysteries. The latter seemed a little awkward all things considered.

'The police told me I'll have to stay for at least forty eight hours, they're speaking to residents, Joanne...'

They knew Joanne wasn't involved, but she might even have seen the man Nick had come across. The pool guy. He wondered where he had even stayed, in fact. So many unanswered questions.

'You know I'm here, Ana. I'm going to get coffees and I'll come up. We're pretty happy with the recording, so I can take my foot off, you know.'

Nick even pondered going back to Barcelona with Ana, if things were settled by then. In the kitchen he found Dom and Cammie, working up a kiwi fruit and mango concoction.

'Back on the health kick then?' asked Nick.

'Yeah. We went to bed at 5 o'clock,' said Dom. She turned to display pupils like two polo mints.

'I'd get some shades on guys,' sniggered Nick, a rare occurrence, him being the odd one out.

Nick could see the police car outside, Cammie and Dom chopping some ginger now. Nick took the coffees upstairs and sat on the one seater couch, pulling it near the bed. Ana looked drawn and thoughtful.

'I didn't say much to the police Nick,' she said. 'I certainly didn't mention my uncle's other affairs or anything with Peru or Barcelona. I just hope this doesn't escalate, you know. I will need to talk to my parents. The family will know what has happened. Papa will tell me the situation. And you'll have a new boss...' she said.

Nick had considered what would happen now that the Big Man wouldn't be managing the band. Would they change labels in Europe? Would the label stay open? Nick sat his coffee down.

'We've got this tour coming up Ana. It starts in two weeks. We've even got this in Glasgow, playing the new album beforehand.'

They sat for a few minutes in mostly silence, both aware that the coming months, year, would be a gruelling adventure. Nick got up and decided to put some music on. 'Let's try and stay upbeat,' he mused.

The sound of Guided By Voices echoed through the suite, and for a few minutes everything seemed normal again. Nick opened the window, checking if the police car was still around. He lit a camel in the hope Ana wouldn't notice, but knew she would anyway.

'Ana,' he said, smoke bellowing to the side of his face. 'The Saab is coming. And another car. It's the police again.'

Ana sighed. It felt like they had only just left, although she was awaiting further news. Not that it would be particularly positive whatever the outcome. She'd find out and talk to mama and papa and hopefully arrange to make it back for a funeral service in their district of the city. It really was their district. It would be big news among the shopkeepers and local businesses, most of whom had some affiliation to her uncle, even if bad.

'We'd better go then,' she sighed.

Nick and Ana went downstairs, opening the door to the officers, preempting their arrival. It was Poirot and Dunn again, the same officer and inspector that had interviewed Nick before. In the following car were another two of the officers. Nick wondered where they were staying on the island. 'Good morning officers,' said Nick.

Ana was making coffees. She'd hoped they wouldn't be around for hours again. 'Good afternoon,' said officer Dunn, correcting Nick. On the ball today, thought Nick, smiling.

'How can we help officers? Do come in.' It was Ana now, standing by the door, waiving them inside.

The two officers made their way into the sitting room. Dom and Cammie must have been sleeping off their late night, Nick decided.

'Yes Ms. Fazio, Mr Black...' went the leading officer. 'We've come to discuss the finer details we've gathered surrounding the incident.'

The officers had taken a seat this time, giving a less informal feel to the place. 'So in this briefing, we'd like to tell you about what we've gathered. It's become official from the evidence there was a small explosive device on board the helicopter, I'm afraid.' Ana let out a slight gasp, she wasn't alarmed, but it wasn't the news she'd hoped for. This would inevitably signal all kinds of new issues back in Barcelona. A new chapter for the family. A re-ordering of the association. Of everything.

'What we have gathered, in the shrapnel of the helicopter itself, is explosive resin pointing towards that. As well as various items which shouldn't, wouldn't be, found in these materials.' Nick and Ana sat in silence. What could they say? They were surprised. How could someone have planted a device on the chopper? Ana already knew, however she didn't wasn't to face the music.

'Mr. Black.' It was the other officer. Poirot with the Dictaphone. White moustache and different suit today. 'We need to get a better description of the man you saw around the house. The pool man as you refer to him.'

The PC had whipped out his notepad now. They both stared at Nick.

'We've had a statement from Joanne. She told us a man was frequenting the pub on a few occasions. It sounds very much like the man you also saw.'

The other officer took his turn now. Moving forward. 'Unfortunately Mr. Black, there are no surveillance cameras on the island. So a thorough description would be vital.' Nick was slightly puzzled, having told the officers everything he could remember. 'Yes, sure. Although I have already spoken to you.' Nick thought hard. 'All I can remember was a man, slightly balding. He had medium to tanned skin, so he might have been from another place. He was medium height. He was wearing a green overall, cleaning the pool. Like a handyman overall. A one-piece zip thingy. His face was a bit like that actor guy, Christopher Walken. But maybe a little older.'

Ana coughed suddenly. The two officers took a glance at her. 'Beg your pardon,' she said.

'Sorry, but that's all I can remember. I saw him again once, when he smiled at me through a window when I was getting water…' continued Nick. 'And he'd freaked me out a bit. But I went back to bed. I was dazed, I wasn't concerned.'

The officers had been taking notes, listening closely, nodding occasionally. The suited man spoke now.

'And can you remember any clothing on the second occasion?'

'Yes. Just a black t-shirt. And I remember a wristwatch. It was orange, I think. That's all…' Nick stared into space, wishing he had more to add, but he didn't.

'An orange wristwatch?' said the PC now. 'That's very interesting.' He scribbled on his notes. 'The nice lady from the pub said the same. Regarding the watch. So thank you for sharing that with us Mr. Black.'

'Just call me Nick officers. Nick is fine.'

The officers nodded acceptingly. It was almost official, the man who had hung around had been in some way out to inflict vengeance on Mr. Fazio, The Big Man. Nick and Ana were full of wonder at how this could have happened. But they would never fully know. It was like something from a film or TV series. He thought of Tony Soprano. This was real though.

'Thank you Mr. Black. The information has been useful. Now, we'll be staying on the island for the next twenty four hours at least, so if you have anything to add, anything at all, please let us know.'

The second officer spoke now. 'Unfortunately it seems the man in question may have left the island already, having spoken to the boat master and his son. But we'll continue to follow all leads and investigate the matter for the foreseeable future.'

That was it then, thought Nick. The guys managed to do a

runner off the island already. Ana had been worried for her own safety, so one good thing would be she could relax a little now.

'Thank you officers. Thank you for the information. We'll let you know if we can think of anything else.' Ana was speaking now, in an assuring tone.

Nick merely nodded. He wanted a coffee. A cigarette. Two maybe. The officers gathered their things and made their way toward the door. One spoke lastly.

'We'll have to keep a police vehicle here should you need any assistance. And for your own safety,' he added.

'OK, sir, that's fine...' said Ana.

'Goodbye.' It had been a brief visit, but Nick and Ana could fill Cammie and Dom in on the info. Ana her family likewise.

Ana had spent most of the afternoon on her phone and laptop. She had spoken to various family members, with one call emerged another. Nick felt a little like a human obstacle, and with Cammie and Dom only just up, he decided to head to the local before tea. He could catch up with Joanne and see what her take on it all was. He left a note for Dom and Cammie and walked down to the pub, the sun settling into balmy low dew. He figured he could also gather his thoughts, have a think about everything. Was Ana going to be safe in Barcelona? Should Nick ask her to come away on tour with the band? Who around them was involved? Maybe everyone, he figured. Nothing would surprise him at the moment.

'Hi Joanne. I'm glad you're open, thought I'd pop in for a couple of pints.'

Nick was glad to see Joanne, who was sitting by the door

with Dino, chewing on an old sandal.

'Hey Nick. Have you heard the news? I'm not allowed to say much, but I'm sure he was in here a couple of times. The man.'

There were only two patrons today, chatting about horse racing, by the sound of things. Joanne switched the TV off. The smell of cardboard and old creels still hung in the air. Nick had come to quite like it, finding a homely comfort in its regularity.

'Aye it's crazy Joanne. I cannae say too much either, but I think he's left the island. Wherever he's gone I don't know. The others are up at the barn. Police too, twenty-four seven.'

Nick took a big swig of his pint, trying not to overdo it, seem civilised. He and Joanne sat a minute, both were unsure of what the other could say. Joanne popped the old TV back on.

'Well,' she said moving in closer. 'He came in the first time. And he didn't speak, at all. She was whispering now. 'I thought he was one of the sound guys. He ordered a large scotch. He sounded foreign. Maybe Italian or something. Anyway, he drank about half a bottle in half an hour. He wasn't friendly at all. Left a fifty pound note on my counter and disappeared. Then the second time was just the same. He definitely didnae want to talk to anyone. No crack at all. I didnae like 'im. He looked a tad malevolent, ya ken?'

Nick nodded, glad he and Joanne were back on full Scottish speaking terms too. The others wouldn't understand much had they been there. They both sat a minute, sighing.

'Teddy the Boatman said two men left. Just recently. I can't believe it was that Flavio! He's gone. He disappeared. He was free to go whenever but I expected a goodbye at least. Ungrateful sod'.

Nick raised an eyebrow. Flavio was gone too? The situation

was looking overwhelmingly crooked. But he didn't want to tell Joanne everything. How could he?

'They got on and paid him and the skipper four hundred quid. Four hundred quid!' Joanne said the last sentence as through he'd purchased their boat. 'Clearly in a rush!'

Nick nodded. He was glad the men were away, whoever they were. Things were adding up more now. He ordered another pint. Racing thoughts.

'Anyway, Joanne. I'll maybe speak to you about it later. At a later date'

Nick had noticed another two men come in, so thought probably best to keep it hushed. Joanne enquired about the music, Dom and Cammie. Nick could tell she wanted more info on Mr. Fazio, but didn't mention him. It was all over, hopefully.

He sipped down his last pint and decided to return up the road, maybe cook some dinner.

'Bye Joanne,' he said. 'Come up to the house anytime. In fact, tell your daughter we've got a gig in Glasgow If she wants to come. You too, of course. Guest list.'

'Oooh really?' she said, looking impressed. 'I've not been out dancing for about thirty five years,' she chortled.

'Seriously, it's on the twenty seventh of this month. I would love it if you could come. I'll put you down plus five, just in case you do.'

Nick gave Joanne a hug, he felt to cement their friendship. He took her e-mail address and phone number. As he was leaving Joanne said his name from the bar. Nick turned around slowly.

'Aye,' he said.

She was pointing at the wall. Nick squinted his eyes. He could see a photo. It was the band. Joanne had hung the picture of the band and her on the wall. His heart swelled, and he returned to give her another hug, smiling.

'I knew you were a good lad,' said Joanne. 'Thanks again. For everything.'

Nick was so taken by the gesture. The band would forever be on the wall of the pub now. He almost shed a tear, so left swiftly, giving Dino a big kiss on the head. His tail was flapping and knocking off a dusty old table.

As he approached the house, Nick could make out Ana, Cammie and Dom standing in the kitchen, cooking. There was a strong smell of rosemary and spices that he followed up the driveway.

'Hey guys,' he said, happy that they could all enjoy dinner together, the only drama being the police car sat out front.

The officers didn't even seem to get out, and a new car arrived at around 10 p.m, switching places.

'Hi Nick. I was gonna come down for a Guinness,' said Cammie, 'But I got ambushed into dicing up our beef.'

'That's right,' said Dom, crunching up carrots, 'Keep that away from me.'

They all dug in and Ana acted as the chief chef, dishing out orders on mastering her Spanish stew and garlic potatoes. It smelled amazing, the half bottle of wine left over dished out between Dom and Cammie. Nick had put four Vermouths into the fridge earlier; it wasn't as though they were going to be drunk anytime soon.

Ana was relatively quiet, the others suggesting a board game or films to watch after tea, so as to take away from any gauche chat. Hearing about it all was probably the last thing Ana wanted to do. They all enjoyed the food, Cammie and Nick ladling into the vegetarian version once they'd finished their beef.

'I think I will have to go back to Barcelona on Tuesday evening,' announced Ana. They were all slightly surprised, but understood. Nick felt he should go with her, though it would mean cutting short their stay by a few days. The album was more or less complete, however.

'Yes Ana. Go and see your family. Totally,' said Dom, Nick and Cammie nodding.

'I should come too,' said Nick. 'I will come. We'll have time to finish the album. We've got this show in Glasgow and then it's ahead with the tour after the album is released.'

Dom and Cammie nodded. They didn't seem to mind, they understood. They'd see Nick again in less than week. They'd stay on, the two of them, at the house, it was decided. Nick could feel Ana give him a little kick under the table, and tried not to laugh. Dom and Cammie could keep themselves otherwise occupied. Enjoy the scenery. They all sat round and gathered to watch some movies, a French war film, and an old James Bond. Cammie made popcorn, inventing sachet cones out of folded up pieces of A4. They'd agreed Nick would return with Ana to Barcelona, and meet they'd others for the show in a week. The band would need to rehearse all day the next day. Ana could get packing, and voila. It was all systems go from here.

14

The plane was a little shaky at first. Nick couldn't stand it, turbulence. His hands would become musty. His throat would dry up. Every jolt made his heart thump into his mouth. He downed his mini bottle of wine. Useless piece of shit, he thought.

Ana was sleeping. She'd had a busy week. Visiting her parents. The funeral. Seeing family was a non stop event, it seemed. Then it was time to pack for Glasgow, where she'd see the band perform their new album to a crowd of around six hundred. A fairly intimate gig, these days. The album would be out the following Monday in the UK, followed by a world-wide release a week after. Ana's uncle's team at the label had it all arranged, though sadly the big man wouldn't be there. The plane jolted again.

'Another wine, please. No, two,' said Nick.

He hoped it wouldn't hit a storm gale, that's all he needed. Welcome back, sucker. He had two more valium, washed down with the vinegar-Merlot. He hoped he'd be knocked out soon too. He remembered on a flight to Sweden once, the band were being scuttled around like nuts in a tin can. Nick had almost had an anxiety attack, trays and bags flailing around like stage divers. The plane shook, a little bell-ping sound causing him to rub his neck. He thought of the good times. Joanne at the pub. Making the album. Seeing Ana. Diving off the cliffs. Meeting Mr. Finn. Having him guest on the album. Eating banana loaf to the sound of the Beach Boys. The Batmobil. It had been an adventure, All right. He'd loved every minute of it. He'd been so relaxed there. No chaos. No hustle and bustle. No taxi horns or odours of kebab meat and spilt liquor at 4 A.M. Just fresh sea air and sun; the salt of the earth. He raised a toast to the far Isle, his glass shaking a little with another jolt. He clenched his jaw.

He'd taken his time after the funeral to call Dom and Cammie, who were fine. He'd see them at the show rehearsal and the sound check. He missed them already, though it had merely been a week. He sniggered to himself as he envisioned them alone, watching movies in the house. Eating popcorn, getting to know one another intimately, perhaps. The plane jerked again. No wonder Nick had these reoccurring dreams, he hated flying. He bit his nail a minute. He stretched his limbs. They'd be in Glasgow anytime soon. Showtime. He stared at Ana's ring, imagining their wedding. He never thought he'd get married so young. If ever. She was special though. One of a kind. She really was a true friend, and he would be honoured to call her his wife. 'Cabin crew, prepare for landing' scratched the captain over the tannoy. Nick cracked a smile.

The band had finished the album. It was ready to go. Nick, Dom and Cammie were at the back of the stage. There wasn't much in the way of a backstage area, just a few rooms and corridors. They were deciding on the setlist, the new album in full, peppered with half of the first album throughout. The fans were ravenous to hear it. The first single had charted at number four in the midweek charts, their highest ever. They could hear the crowd from outside, chanting and blowing horns, it sounded like a football match. They'd all forgotten how it felt to play live, it'd been a while. Cammie was looking ashen faced, his leg trembling. He was cradling a beer. He'd only played live at high school, over a decade ago. Dom was doing her usual pacing, jumping small jumps on the spot occasionally, twisting her wrists to get them elasticised. They'd lined up their trademark three shots of single malt, one each before showtime. The whistles, commotion and noise were building. The band could hear their playlist over the sound system, a mix of their favourite songs. Cammie had popped his drumsticks into his back pocket now. Ana would be watching from the side of the stage, along with their PR people, family, and assorted management.

'Right guys, you're on ASAP. So good luck, eh.'

It was a stagehand, a bald man covered in sweat. They all exchanged glances. The sound of Weezer's 'Island In the Sun' was fading out slowly. They all had a large shot each, and exchanged hugs to soothe the burning.

'Go for it Cammie,' said Nick. 'They're gonna love you'.

'Let's do this!' shouted Dom, a freshly dyed streak of violet covering one eye.

They huddled at the side of the stage, as they usually did. Dom sometimes didn't look out, after she once experienced stage fright at a gig in Brixton. Nick was shaking a little. He peeped out of the curtain at the crowd, camera phones flashing like tiny cluster bombs of white light. He took in the front rows, squashed together and chanting. Suddenly he stopped, His legs went weak. Blood drained from his head. It was like a snare drum had been struck into his brain. There they were, the window cleaning man, together with Flavio, in the middle of the front row, together. They stood completely still, dressed in all black. Deadly sombre, they stared back. Nick felt an overwhelming rush of sickness and nerves, which almost made him recoil. His mouth was agape.

'Dom! Dom!' he shouted. 'This isn't funny, it's Flavio and the window guy, they're…'

Both men had raised a hand each, displaying the same sign his sidekick had made at Nick and Ana on the Island. It was a message. A coded family sign. The pair stared at Nick with evil eyes and coolly turned and disappeared into the crowd, gone into the night.

'That's it. It's time pal. That's it, it's time.'

Nick gulped down and the stagehand had his arm. Dom and Cammie were about to go on. He heard a roar go up, Cammie and Dom were seconds from the stage. His mind and body were overdosing on adrenaline. Racing thoughts. Racing thoughts.

Cammie moved first. Applause. The crowd knew they had a new drummer. Building, a slow tidal wave of noise. Dom now. Camera. Flashes. More screams. She had lifted her bass, a beautiful powder blue Fender Mustang. Nick now. He walked toward his guitar. He often felt like he was walking backwards going on stage, for some reason. Blinding red lights. The heat, intense like a burning war zone. Flags. People on shoulders. Rumbling waves of noise. He strapped on his guitar, his trusty old Fender Telecaster. He'd put a new tiny Scottish flag on the fretboard. Screaming. Shouting. A pint cup flying. He glanced very quickly at the balcony. He could see lots of familiar faces. He strummed a single chord.

'Hello you.' A cheer. A flying beer.

'We've been away for a while, making *Sophomore Songs*. Nice to see you all.'

He crunched down on a G chord. A trickle of sweat rolled down his neck.

'This is a new song from the album; it's called *Joanne*.'

A huge cheer went up. Dom was pointing at the balcony. Nick etched his head upwards. It was her. It was Joanne. She was glowing. Her daughter stood beside her, smiling and hugging Joanne. It was chaotic already. Bodies surging toward the stage like an ebbing tide. Strobe lights. Nick started the riff. God, he'd missed this. A flare now, at the back. AWOL. Nick turned to Cammie. Cammie was sweating. Dom was jumping on the spot. 'And a one, two, a-one-two-THREE-FOUR...'

PART TWO

15

The band were sat out on the rooftop veranda in Barcelona's business district. This was DiDi Papaz, recently voted the city's most pretentious eatery by a leading food critic. The menu, made up of truffle foams and Iberico-shaved aubergine, had the phallus puns running wild. Ana was on the phone, looking unimpressed.

'Yes. Five minutes? Oh. Goodbye.'

She snapped her phone shut and looked at the band. 'He's coming. Fix up, guys.'

They were waiting for their new label boss, Don Cechil, Ana's second uncle and youngest brother to Fazio and her trouble reluctant father. He'd recently decamped from Peru to Europe, and the band had heard murmurs, rumours of a dangerous but fragile figure that supposedly once attempted to bite off a rival's finger. He was to be approached with caution. To make matters worse, Ana had only met him twice.

'Please, everyone behave,' she cautioned. 'And do not call him "Don", OK?

He won't like this type of language, and neither do I'

'Ana, I don't even know what's going on anymore. I can't get hold of most of the team. You know, our agent, the PR, organisers, the lot. What are you on about the "Don" for? Dom was irate; Nick and Cammie felt it brewing.

'Everyone just chill, we're going on tour, it's gonna be fun. All right?'

Cammie was happy to play peacekeeper; he'd dealt with

some of the industry's most peculiar characters, after all.

Ana had given them some info. Cechil had resided in Cusco and ran business there up until recently. Often cited as one of the friendliest nationalities in the world, it didn't sound as though he had brought much of the Peruvian spirit back to his birthplace. He was taking over Fazio's leg of the machine in Spain – this meant he was their new boss. Not only their boss, but that of all operations in Barcelona and beyond.

Ana had met him as a teen and then recently at Fazio's funeral, where he'd made a drunken yet poetic speech. He'd ended the evening dancing with a well-known Spanish model before exiting in an armoured vehicle.

Cammie had removed his cap, anxiously popping it under the table. Ana folded her necktie, and Dom cleared her throat. Nick had been short on conversation generally, gnawing on his fingernails in the searing sun. He tended to do this more often whilst on tour, but the band never mentioned it.

A walk-in lift made a ping sound, like a microwave producing a heated piranha.

Two black-clad men swiftly exited the elevator, followed by a further two, rather burly-looking thugs in black puffer Jackets. They perused the scene. Guests were swaying their heads to get a look, possibly expecting a Spanish actor or film director.

The staff began whispering among themselves. The men waived him in.

Through the gang strolled a plain black suit, with clinking black shoes shining like a newly oiled bald patch. It was Don Cechil. He didn't seem overly menacing or what they'd expected, but then, who was.

He walked slowly toward the table, shades glimmering against the sun. He had a slight slant in his walk. A toothpick and a ruby handkerchief were neatly tucked into his suit. A thin scar on his left cheek ran up to his shades, perhaps even further. Some gunmetal grey stubble hid a sneering lip. On closer inspection, he did ooze a certain power, or confident command.

Cammie and Nick caught one another's eye, mystified at the amount of random personnel around this guy. Nick did realize he hadn't told Dom and Cammie quite what was going on at the moment, just that there was to be a reshuffling at the label.

He just wanted it over with; he had the fear at the best of times.

'Ana,' purred Cechil calmly, taking her hand and bowing his head.

'My child from the Europas.'

The band all smiled, as did Ana. Dom took it further by giving Nick a dunt under the table. She wasn't in the mood for grandiose introductions. She crossed her eyes and slipped her tongue out through the right side of her cheek. She looked slightly deranged.

Nick let out a snort. He couldn't hold it. His nostrils flared and made a minor farting burst, causing him to choke a little. As he looked up, he saw Cechil staring blankly at him. His head was unmoving. His face was entirely vacant. He continued to stare for an agonising four, five seconds in silence, and not a muscle moved. The table shared a tone of acute anxiety. He wasn't happy.

'Usually,' he said, moving his napkin to one side. He took off his shades and placed them on the table. His scar ran further up his stubble cheek, right to his eye. He stared at the band now.

'When a man owes me eighty thousand euros, they don't smile so hard.'

Nick's well-meaning smile slowly drooped into a wincing, upended croissant shape.

Dom wished she hadn't tried lighting the mood. Ana and Cammie exchanged glances.

'Bahahaha.' He let out a manic laugh and brashly elbowed Ana, who was sitting next to him. His men began chortling along, one by one. The Mook Brigade, as the band had gotten to calling them. Nick felt a rush of relief, as did Ana. He even mustered a smile again.

'I am just breaking bread.' He brushed his shoulder as if removing dirt.

'I am Cechil, your new boss. Ana can fill you in.'

Nick and Dom let out sighs of relief, and Cammie was taking in the scene as if playing a bit-part in a Spanish TV drama. The Barca loner, perhaps. Ana nodded pleasingly, and the band followed suit.

'So, I hear you have a valuable new album under your skinny jeans, no? So, this is what we do…' The band had all turned, closely awaiting more. Their fate, perhaps.

'You guys tour from now until Christmas.' He made a chopping motion on the table, as if moving from one Country to the next.

'All over. You talk to me once a month. We have a meeting. You get to have fun, see the world, and you pay back my mullah as soon as you have done enough shows.'

'Your label mates will be a new signing, Ze Conks. I have also set up a very lucrative set of shows in July with them.'

The band exchanged glances and panicked a little. The

Conks? Surely not. The pop-punk borderline boyband with Johnny Jah as a lead vocalist? That gak-addled, fame-ravenous, wannabe Love Island contestant? Oh, Christ. Oh no. The band sat in silence. Even Ana was surprised when they'd signed to the label recently. They must be going for the big time in Europe, she figured.

A cloud of upset frittered through the group; part bemusement, equal parts dread.

Nick took a chance now. 'Sir, Mr Cechil, if I could just…'

'Ok. Now, I am not like my brother, my dearest Fazio. I do not care about music. I find it upsetting. I care about mullah— the dough. Loot. The bread and honey. *Capisce?* Good.'

He snorted his left nostril hard and broadened his shoulders.

Don't care about music? What are we doing sat here? Screamed Dom, in her head.

'Now, which of you two shloppaz is marrying my niece?'

Don Cechil's pronunciation of the letters 'S' and 'T' rolled off his tongue like a 'Z'. Much like a Frenchman, thought Dom. Nick was confused about everything. He just wanted the album out, his baby. The band's shining trophy for the future.

'I am, sir. I'm Nick. Pleased to meet you.'

'U huh. And you, Neeek.' He nodded.

He clicked his fingers and motioned an aide, who swiftly produced five flutes of champagne to the table.

Ana looked a little embarrassed. He hadn't even given the band a chance to speak.

'A celebration,' he raised his glass, 'to ze future.' They all clinked and tried to smile, a little lost for words, frankly.

'Your new manager will be here in a minute. He is busy arranging some sort of grunge makeovers for Ze Conks. Divas…'

162

'New manager? What? Hold on…' Nick was suddenly irate, and Ana put her glass down. 'Uncle, what new manager? The band likes to work on their own term…'

-'Hush your mouth, my sweet child,' said Cechil in a creepily quiet voice, cutting Ana off mid-sentence. 'You need a manager. He is one of the best. I had my men do my homework. We are going for the big time. I even listened to your album on the plane.'

He looked back toward the band. 'It sounds like my brother made a good investment. The mullah will flow like wine,' he remarked, removing his toothpick.

He put down his glass. He had darker skin than Fazio had; perhaps it was the Peruvian climes.

'Mr Cechil. May I add?' Dom had taken the courage to speak up. Nick and Cammie were relieved. Ana, knowing better, stayed silent for the time being. She'd be speaking to Don Cechil later about family matters.

'I'm not sure we need a manager. And us touring with The Conks, I'm really not su…'

'Hush now, my girl. It is a very good move. You could buy a house in London. A new frock. In any case, as I was saying…'

He waived his wrist as if swatting a pesky mosquito. A diamond shone from his pinkie ring, catching the sun.

'A new frock? What are you talki-'

'Look, if you want to go and sign to Backwaters records on the eve of your tour, then do it.' The Don had cut in swiftly, ghosting Dom in the process.

'But you're taking my debt with you. So, now that that's settled, I do hope you will enjoy your time on the road. I will see you soon. And, I will talk to Ana about our little problem.

163

The problem you had on the island with these impostors. It will not happen again. We will settle this the old way. For my dear Fazio…'

He picked up a napkin and dabbed his cheek, and took a moment of reflection.

'My Dear Fazio. To revenge. Venganza por la familia!' he screamed. He'd raised a glass. 'Veganza!' shouted his aides, in tandem, like a militia.

The staff all whispered some more, and a table of women looked on fretful.

What had just happened here? Nick bit at a fingernail. The whole team around the band had somehow disappeared overnight. Sacked, fed to Universal Credit.

The band was indebted to a new source, jeopardising most of their future decisions, so it seemed. Dom was scowling to herself, Nick had noted. Cammie and Ana could feel certain despair in the air. In times past, they would probably just nip to the toilet one by one, making light of the situation. But after finishing their album, a pact had been made; no nose blasts on the road.

Suddenly, the lift pinged, and a tall, wrangler wearing man strolled onto the rooftop. His chest was puffed out; looking not unlike Dustin Hoffman in *Midnight Cowboy*. He lit up a cigarette before approaching the table. He was older than expected, in his late fifties, perhaps. He had a cheek full of gum. Or tobacco.

'Aha. This is my guy now. This man is a pro, children. His name is Kilo.'

'Kilo?' said Dom, shaking her head.

'Hey, Gang. How do, Mr. Ceceel.'

The man took a seat and removed his hat. 'Bitch of a flight. Thank god for Librium. Can I get a beer around here?' he barked at a waiter.

Cammie knew instantly he was from the U.S, he recognised his southern style as possibly Texan. Thoroughbred Americana, whoever he was. He twirled a caviar-covered breadstick and shrugged his shoulders at Nick.

'I'm a little short on time. And time is money, Mr Ceceel.'

Don stared at the man as if he was a foreign object. Or a freshly dropped dog turd, perhaps. Then, he slowly began to smile.

'I like your way of thinking, Kilo. But, show some manners. Do you have a problem pronouncing my name? What is this?'

Cechil rubbed his index finger up and down against his lips, as though to show contempt for Kilo's speech. He muttered something in his native Catalonian, but the word 'Americans' was audible.

'So anyway, this is the band and my beautiful niece Ana. She assures me the band have made a chart-burning CD, which we will release. You will take care of them all on Tour. OK?'

'Hello, gang,' he went, perusing the band. 'I'm your new manager. Forget your other team. It's Kilo or the highway from now on. No hissy fits up in my grill, ya hear? Or I'll ship you back to Harry Potter land quicker than you can strum a bum note.'

The band laughed genuinely and awkwardly. Was this guy for real?

Cechil stood up slowly and took Ana's hand. He stared at the band as if hopeless sheep.

'It was a pleasure to meet you all. And you are a pretty one, aren't you?' He glanced at Dom. Her new purple fringe had caught his eye. She wriggled a little in her seat. She couldn't stand these people, let alone understand what was going on.

'Kilo has your touring schedule. Have fun, and break a leg or two. It's all media mullah for me. Bye, children.'

'Hey, Ceceeel!' shouted Kilo as Don made his way across the rooftop. Cechil turned his head and peered back at the table.

'What about my contract? Four hundred thou, one year, yeah?'

The band was all ears. Half a million? To this guy? Smite me down, thought Nick. They'd never even had a manager before. They'd survived on a thirty euro per-head budget in Europe for an entire year.

'Be calm, Kilo. Be calm. You will get your money as soon as we all do.'

Don walked on, murmuring. He spoke quietly to his aides in Spanish. 'You bag of rats piss.' They chortled along toward the lift.

Kilo looked furious. He grabbed his Stetson and got up. One remaining man took hold of his shoulder and pushed him back down. 'No wise,' he cautioned Kilo.

'Would you be damned?' Kilo said in his Texan twang. 'What a f…'

He looked at Ana and closed his mouth. He took a mammoth gulp of beer. Foam dripped down his chin. 'All right guys. Don't worry. You'll get to know me; I like to act the clown, but don't cross the line. I'm a nice guy really. Now here's your schedule. I will be with you every few days.' A pager made a beeping sound around his waist. 'I gotta go. The Conks guy is throwing chairs at the walls. Someone took his necktie or some shit. But, any problems at all just call me. Here's my business card. I'll see you in two days, on the tour bus. I ain't travellin' gypo style, though. Hell Nah. Strictly first class for me.'

He produced four sheets of A4, jam-packed with tour dates and the names of accommodations under each one. It read like an atlas, producing a mix of sighs, guffaws, and shrieks around the table.

'You'll have a ball. I'm here to keep you happy and outta trouble. So saddle up, kids. Time to dig for some gold.'

He devoured his beer and power walked to the lift, muttering swear words to himself, presumably aimed at Cechil. Nonetheless, he had a friendly demeanour about him, they'd conceded. Almost buffoonish, but knowingly. Deliberately.

Nick sat forward. 'Can you imagine two people more different to those two?

Dom and Cammie shook their heads. Dom was still reeling from it all.

'Is this what happens when you have a bit of success? It's just an unsystematic ladder of increasingly eccentric, random characters?'

'I guess so, it is in my experience,' added Cammie, not looking too fazed by it all.

'I think this Kilo guy's actually pretty funny. I would take him with a pinch of salt.'

'A pinch? A fucking Kilo indeed,' went Nick, chewing a pinky nail.

'Firstly, I'm sorry, guys. I feel like I got you into this mess. I'm glad the label is staying in the family, though.'

Ana was anxious, hoping the band would go easy on her. Nick was on edge, staring into his empty champagne flute. He wished he was back on the island, getting high, listening to his old records, visiting Joanne, walks along the coastline.

'It's OK, Ana. What can we do? We got our advance on the album. Hopefully, it'll do well.'

'I know,' went Dom. 'Let's just try and enjoy ourselves. At the end of the day, it's the band and you, Ana. That's the gang. And hopefully, we can pay back your uncle in a few months and make the most out of our time. We've all worked hard to get here, so don't forget that. Sometimes in life, you have to zoom out a little and realise what's important.'

Cammie and Nick both turned to Dom. She had read their thoughts. She'd somehow recaptured the spirit of the band. The gang. The last survivors in town.

'Would sirs care for the nine-course experience today? Mr Cechil has pre-paid.'

A suited waiter had approached and was fake-smiling over the table.

Nick shrugged his shoulders and looked at the others.

'May as well. We've got a lot to discuss.'

Ana and Nick knew the time had also come to tell the others. It was becoming too awkward to bear, and life on the road would only get harder keeping secrets. Nick wanted it all out in the open; he'd made a conscious decision not to keep anything from his bandmates in the future. They rode the storms together.

'So. I will get around to the tour and everything later. But me and Ana,' he scratched his neck, 'Ana and I have to tell you something.'

They both held hands, though rather awkwardly. This

meeting had become a thing of great importance for the band on many levels. Dom and Cammie were a little lost.

'Wait, are you pregnant?' shrieked Dom, clapping her hands.

'Oh no, no, Dom,' said Ana swiftly. 'But it is about my family...'

The waiter placed four tiny bowls around the table. The first course was a white, egg-shaped ball of something. Nobody knew what exactly, but all smiled.

Ana and Nick proceeded to explain everything slowly and cautiously. The whole back story. The drama on the island. Their new label boss. Whether they liked it or not, they were all, on some level, involved.

'I knew it!' went Cammie. 'I told you before, Nick. These cats were different...'

'Can today get any stranger?' was Dom's response. 'I'm not sure it can.'

'So then Nick and I saw the man gesture toward us with his hands on the island. I knew then something was amiss. It was the sign of an old, rival family: The Pachos. Then the 'window cleaning man' and him turned up at your concert. And obviously, it was a warning. They got rid of Fazio and are looking to take over the business. So be careful. And tell me if anything happens.'

'Be careful?' Dom and Cammie urged. 'We just want to play music'

Nick was shaking his head; it was still almost unfathomable to him too. His dedication toward Ana, however, who had helped him through so many rough times, was unwavering. The talk went on through all nine courses, some of which were merely a thimble of rustic painted nuts doused in plumes of smoky, herbal air. An artform, they all agreed.

Ana suddenly got an incoming call; it was her Uncle Cechil directly this time. She took a pen from her bag and scribbled an address on a napkin.

'Ok, uncle. Nick and I will be there in one hour. Bye.'

Her uncle had called to arrange a reunion with the two. He informed them to be wary of anyone following them and be on the lookout. Ana thought him to be overly paranoid. They said their goodbyes and headed to the nearest underground station.

The band was set to regroup in two days, starting in Milan, according to their schedule. The excitement was building. An air of adventure was mounting between them. The album was hitting the shelves tomorrow, and it was time to hit the road.

16

Nick was quiet in the balmy underground. He popped an extra med before lunch, hoping it would keep him calm. He was taking in the graffiti mostly, the scents of carcinogenic grease and fast food vendors. For some reason, it brought back many memories of the band's early days, hopping around Europe without a care in the world. It was bordering on a backpacker's holiday, their measly budget stretching to the occasional city tour or the odd bag of whatever pick-me-up was available (bar the heavy stuff). They'd survive on fruit and proteins. Dom was occasionally lucky enough to flirt her way into a hot meal from one of her growing fanbase, mostly teenage boys. It was ironic, as, at the time, she was in contemplation about her sexuality and wasn't likely to sleep with anyone, let alone a couple of male fans. But never mind, the odd Pizza and lunch menu helped them out a lot. Nick wondered if anything was happening between Cammie and her, as they still seemed very close and had left lunch together. He figured he'd see over time. He would be made up for Dom if she met a music-loving soul mate, and Cammie definitely had the right character. He was one of the only people Nick had met who understood the mechanisms of his musical brain. Ana was reading her books on the underground, having arranged a working tour sabbatical to accompany the band's tour.

The smell of grime, sewage and clipped air on the underground was becoming a bit much for Nick. His senses were always heightened in the city. He was daydreaming about how many crowds they'd be playing to. The mere thought made his heart pound.

They reached their stop and bounded out into the sunny city street, aligned with trees and a ukulele-strumming busker. Families ate tapas outside cafes. Stray city dogs darted between old rusty Renaults. Ana fumbled around for the hotel address she'd taken down, which luckily was right on the corner. Very plush yet discreet.

They got up to the suite, impressed with the hotel's corridors. Spanish art lined the walls, and lush plants sprouted in symmetrical lines.

They could see one of the aides outside the door, so knew where to go instantly.

'Come in, Nick, Ana.' Her uncle opened the door wide and beckoned them into the sitting room. It was more of a flat than a hotel suite. Marble statues, Flatscreen TVs, and huge couches made up the sitting room. An aide was sitting on the balcony, presumably baking alive. The Don seemed far more at home here.

'I wanted to talk to you two properly. Get to know you. You are family, after all.

Do you like Gelato? This is my favourite, Pistachio and Rum. There's coffee on the table.'

Ana and Nick had taken a seat and were facing Cechil. A huge window looked out onto the east of the city. They hadn't expected to see him so soon. He was certainly more relaxed than before.

'I had to see you quickly. I am mostly in transit at the moment. I move hotel every day. I have five cell phones. I'm incognito. A ghost.'

He stirred his espresso with a miniature spoon and looked at the pair.

He scooped some ice cream into his mouth. 'Wonderful.'

'Nick. It is important that you understand the ways of the family. Firstly, are you interested in money?' He dropped his glasses down a little and caught sight of Nick.

'Erm, well, aye, as much as the next man, I guess. But no, not really, sir. I just want to be able to make musi…'

'Can I tell you two a funny story about money? A lesson I learned at a young age.' He'd cut Nick off again. This seemed to be a hobby of Don's. Nick could see the similarities between Fazio and his brother creeping in now.

'I had saved my money one summer. I was around ten years old. I spent the summer sweeping my father's bistro and running errands. I made quite a lot—a chunk, perhaps. So, at the end of the summer, my father took me in his car to buy a Gelato. I loved that car. Anyway, I had all my money in my shirt. But I got scared, and I stuffed it all into my seat, hoping nobody would notice. We got the ice cream, and we went back to the car. After I finished, I quickly remembered the money and put my hand down the seat—it was all gone. I was destroyed. I was so angry. In tears…'

He put his fist against his heart. He looked at them both. 'My papa, you see, had taken it.'

He sat back. His lip lifted to one side in remembrance. 'Then he turned to me, and he say, 'Son, always, always know where your money is,' and he threw it all back at me, notes flying everywhere.'

Nick and Ana took in the tale, perhaps some wise future advice, who knows. This was definitely Fazio territory now.

'So, Nick, always know where your money is. I had your books looked at. Your team of 'friends' were making a small fortune from the band. So, I'll handle things from here, and trust me, you will be a rich man soon.'

Nick didn't know whether to take it as a compliment, a threat, or an offering. He wasn't about to argue, that was for sure. 'All right, sir, well, that would be… nice, I suppose…' He glanced at Ana and made a little shrug of a shoulder.

'Yes. Yes, Nick. It will be nice, as you say. Now, about the two men you saw on the Scottish island. Is this them?'

He slid an old photograph across the table. It was a faded portrait of Fazio, himself, Ana's father, and the two men from the island, smiling together around a table. They all looked so much younger. It made Ana smile initially, but then her anger grew.

'Definitely.'

'I thought as much. They are treacherous boot lickers. Lamebotas. They are seniors with the Pachos Gang. They have been wading on our turf for a decade but have grown some real cohunes recently. The Brothers Black. I will get them soon. Now, I must go. I have a meeting across town. I will see you both in a month. Enjoy Europe. It's on me.'

Cechil stood up and ushered them out of the room. Ana gave him a hug and bowed her head upon leaving. Nick still felt like a scavenger, his beat-up Converse and ruffled hair looking thoroughly out of place.

They made their way across the city back to their apartment. They felt a little more at ease now and were discussing their trips to Denmark, Sweden, Czech, and later, further a field. Milan was first up. Shit, better get some new shoes, thought Nick...

'Thank you, Italia!' screamed Nick, drenched in sweat. He'd ripped his t-shirt at the neck and was nursing a cut on his leg from mounting the drumkit. Dom's amp had taken a battering, too, grating her bass against the metal box amid a sea of strobes and feedback. They'd played a blinder, and the album was racing up the charts to a respectable number six. Cammie shimmered out his cymbals while standing, then collapsed over his drum stool. They walked off to the roaring of satisfied fans. Italians had grown to love them for some reason. A recent review in European Rolling Stone had called the new album a 'Tour De Force of gritty rock n roll', which had made them all smile in private.

Their dressing room was noticeably nicer than they'd previously had. No pen-covered walls dabbed in obscenities from other bands. No lukewarm beer crates and cigarette-burned seats buckled on the ground. It actually didn't stink.

'That was it, guys! You rocked out.' It was Kilo, sounding like John Wayne-meets-Alan Partridge. He was in high spirits, having learned of the band's chart placing. He'd been surveying its climb to the top daily, like a child's calendar nearing Christmas day. All he needed now was to break The Conks, and he could buy himself a huge ranch, sit on his perch, and listen to Hank Williams. To hell with these cowboys.

'Aye, right on, Kilo,' said Nick, as champagne sprayed against his cheek. Cammie was hyper. It frothed over them all like an effervescent volcano.

'Yeah, it was fun. If all the shows are like this, we'll be making our mark by the end of the year.'

'Attaboy.' He patted the others on the shoulders.

Dom and Cammie were wiping themselves down with a pile of fresh towels by the dressing table. Whether it was his accent or slightly comedic demeanour, the band found it hard to take Kilo seriously, though he had grown on them. Ironically, he made endless jibes about Nick and Dom being British, as though he felt the same way about them. He and Cammie got on surprisingly well, mocking each other's regional accents.

'Whoa. That was a rush. I can't wait to play again tomorrow. This is the life for me, one hundred percent.' Cammie was still somewhat shaken by the levels of adrenaline pounding his heart. He was acclimatising to life on the road, slowly but surely.

'You did great, Cammie. Let's get back to the bus'

Nick and Dom were grabbing their personal items; they didn't see much point in hanging around backstage. Their fans had been out front. Dom also knew to keep an eye on Nick whilst on tour. His moods could differ, and his anxiety levels could worsen like a black veil of melancholy. She knew drugs wouldn't help long term. But he seemed to be enjoying it so far and coping without the marching powder.

'Now, hold on just a second, bucko.' It was Kilo. He sauntered over to the trio for some last words, a clipboard in his hand. 'I got to run down a few things.'

'Tomorrow, we do a roll call in Lyon. You guys have to be up at 8 AM. There's press with two TV stations. One filmed out in the country. Now I don't care what you do after that. Sniff a half-ounce of weed killer. Kick Paparazzi. Sign a contract to sell fungus remover. As long as you're on time for your press junkets, old Kilo boy stays happy. If not, then we got a problem. And if we got a problem, my high-heeled Ropers will send you back to the coalface with Mr. Bean faster than you can spell Indie-pop, ya hear?'

The band was shaking their heads, laughing and shrugging their shoulders.

'Now go on now, have a good night. I'm goin' to get me a pizza the action.'

Kilo and sauntered out with a smirk on his face. They'd figured out he enjoyed acting some kind of caricature of a Southern music mogul.

The metal doors of the arena slammed open, the cold air hitting them one by one.

It led them almost straight onto their tour bus. It was a palatial night liner that resembled a four-star hotel inside. Each bunk boasted duck duvets, built-in screens, and tiny fridges for each member. The sitting area at the rear looked like a miniature nightclub. Almost what they'd imagined a high-end bordello might be like. Cammie had begun collecting pictures of Peter Stringfellow for the walls, and other memorabilia. It was the Batmobil all over again.

The band collapsed into the corner couch, and the bus engines started up. Ana eventually jumped aboard, coming straight from the balcony section.

'That was fantastic, guys. France, tomorrow. Let's see what we can do after the press jobs.'

Cammie looked over at them; he was deadbeat. His ears hummed a distant yet constant pitch of a high violin note. Dom had almost nodded off in her bra. Looking for his tablets, Nick was the colour of a scarlet sausage. He put on Lou Reed's 'Berlin' and early Stevie Wonder as the bus got an early departure. Good going for day one, they agreed.

17

'OK – Nick, now you go right. Slightly more to the right. Dom, give us a pout, darling. That's right, sugar.' Snap. Click, snap. 'Smile.' Snap. Click.

'No, not so much. But do smile. Smile like you're British.'

'What? We are British,' whispered Dom at the side of her mouth, posing on a cliff on the French Riviera. It was a PR job for a Parisian Fashion mag, and the band had all agreed to wear what they were told—a fine selection of leather jackets.

'A bit better than my first old uniform for cleaning hotels,' jibed Nick.

'And mine, selling mixtapes on my block after school. No uniform, though.'

The band laughed as a swarm of media personnel hummed and hawed around them.

'I'm keeping this jacket you know,' went Dom. 'Probably worth more than my bass guitar.'

'Yeah, and then some,' said Nick, also pointing out that Cammie looked not unlike Andre3000. 'Huh?' He shrugged, feeling the heat in the sun. 'Nah, a young Tony Williams from Miles Davis' band,' said Dom, to which he was more impressed.

Ana was waving at the three from inside the bus, still working on her books and editing, but loving the character of the rustic French countryside.

'Ok, guys, that's a wrap. Thank you all, and enjoy La Françoise.'

The theatrical, moustachioed photographer had been irate since he arrived. His editor had threatened his job if he didn't deliver with the pictures pronto.

'What, that's it? We're getting paid to stand on a hillside wearing leather for an hour? Shit, sign me up'.

'Yeah, Cammie. It's ridiculous. Such is life. And we've got the rest of the day to ourselves.'

The band had arranged to stop off at a famous French winery, followed by a trip to the local Aqua Park. They could care less about photo shoots and silly interviews, but it was part of the job. Keep Don Cechil and Kilo happy enough to see the world, record albums, and listen to music—that was the goal.

The bus clanged down the mountainside as the band got seated around the table.

It was stunning. All French elegance: rolling hillsides, chalets, and cafes. Plum trees and medieval churches, bicycle bells, and flat-capped farmhands. 'It's so pretty.'

EEEEkkk! The bus careered across the road suddenly. There was a bang from the front end. The horn blasted out violently. They all jolted forward; Nick's palets de dame flew through the air and scudded off the window. The bus had made an emergency stop at the side of a verge. The driver, a colossal seal of a man named Tubo, was shouting obscenities only Ana could understand. The band exchanged tandem glances in fright, and the bus doors opened. 'What the hell!' shouted Cammie. 'Would you watch where you're goin' Tubo!' came Nick, clotted cream on his chin from the cake.

Suddenly, out of a black MPV blocking the front of the bus stepped two men. Nick and Ana quickly got to the window.

They were surprised none of them was injured. It was them. The wayward assassins. Joanne's so-called gardener and the pool guy. They were back, and they were after something.

'Nick, it's them,' cautioned Ana, her mouth slightly agape. 'It's the Brothers.' Nick peeled some remnants of cream from his fringe. 'It is. Oh shit.'

Dom had taken her sleeping bag as if preparing to hide somewhere, and Cammie took hold of her right hand in fright. They were approaching the bus.

'Don't say anything, anyone. Just be calm,' went Ana, herself shaken and fretful.

The two horrid hombres sauntered past the driver without a care in the world. He was too large to take any action, shouting from his driver's cubicle at the front. One of the men pulled out a black, cosh-like small bat and whacked him on the shoulder hardly. He fell silent in fright. The other man, the window cleaner guy Nick had recognised, had pulled out a very small pistol and was holding it toward the ground. The band, and Ana, were suddenly terrified. It was as if things were moving in slow motion in Nick's head. Be it the utter anxiety or adrenaline, he'd felt this before—on stage.

'You, Ana.' He waived the dark metal poking out of his wrist, a shining silver barrel popping out of his black suit. 'We have a message for your uncle. You tell him we are back. And we are taking over. You understand? You stupid little girl. My boss is coming for your family, putas.'

He lifted the pistol, and a loud shot banged against a glass pane on the window. They all jumped simultaneously. None of them knew what to do. Ana's mouth had dried up. She couldn't swallow. Nick was shaken, as were the others. There was a collective ringing in the ears, like a clap had been amplified a thousand times.

'Leave us alone,' shouted Dom suddenly. 'Just stay away.'

Nick and Cammie nodded their heads. The men turned and were off the bus within seconds, laughing between themselves. Glass particles had sprayed onto the leather seats of the bus. Tubo, who had managed to get out now, wasn't quick enough to reach their car. God forbid he had, for he may have caught a stray one himself.

The group all looked at one another as the black MPV screeched down the hill, leaving black tyre marks following its rapid descent. The air stunk of cologne and sulphuric gunpowder residue.

'I'm sorry, guys. I'm so sorry.' Ana was sobbing slightly, her hands shaking. 'This won't happen again.'

'This shit's crazy,' pondered Cammie aloud, somewhat soberly. Tubo was making sure they were all OK. 'Aye, Cammie, it's been a whirlwind so far,' nodded Nick, dumbfounded and picking fragments of glass from his leather jacket. 'Why does this stuff always happen to us? I feel like calling it a day, I honestly do.'

Dom was silent, grief stricken, perhaps.

'Well, I hope this water park's a good laugh,' came Cammie. Dom and Ana shook their heads at him. He got up and looked out at the scenery. 'Anyone for a beer…?'

It was early, 9 AM. The band had been ordered to an emergency Zoom call with Don Cechil. The mix of dramas and vertical waterslides had left them all shell-shocked from the day before. Ten pit stops for shots at the pool bar hadn't helped.

'I've placed an extra man on the bus. He is coming shortly. He will join Tubo at the front. He is one of my finest men, a Moldovan ju-jitsu champion. Harder than a cannonball. You will be safe. Just don't piss him off. I am moving hotels today, but I will keep in touch. Enjoy the delights of Sweden, children.'

The laptop screen went dead, and the band sat around the table, wishing they could converse more with Cechil. Straighten out the chaos, perhaps. Nick's anxiety levels were in flux, so he'd decided to make some coffee and put on some Hole in an attempt to lighten the mood. The landscape had changed overnight, and a few windmills and big, boldly coloured wooden houses peppered the flat landscape.

'Look,' said Ana suddenly. She turned her phone screen toward the band. 'The album's at No.3 in Europe, number 2 in the UK!'

'Wow,' shouted Cammie, 'that's fantastic.' Dom had taken the phone to make sure she heard correctly. They really were doing well, better than ever before. The first record had been a creeper on the charts. This one, however, seemed to be an altogether different beast.

'Oh gosh,' blushed Nick. 'That's wild, man.' His Glaswegian accent always seemed to come to the fore when he was surprised. 'I guess we're pop stars,' he deadpanned.

'Nick,' said Ana, elbowing his somewhat puny frame. 'Don't be such a pessimist. It's brilliant.'

The bus made a stop at a roadside café and luxury resort to pick up Kilo. He'd flown in the night before. Tubo had boarded up the window overnight, hoping it would stay sealed.

'Hey. I didn't think y'all would be up. What do they teach

you at rock n roll high these days? Pie charts and goddamn elocution lessons? He'd changed into a different plaid shirt, the sprouting of a goatee amassing on his face.

'Anyways, I heard you've been havin' some problems. I talked with Mr. Ceceel, and he's put this nice gentleman on the bus with you guys. It seems Ceceel has some enemies, by the looks of things.'

An extremely athletic man in a vest and sleeveless bomber jacket had taken a seat at the front opposite Tubo. He turned to the band, giving a blank nod.

'Hey also - you guys are smashin' up the charts. Congrats. The last time I was on the road with such a successful act, Donnie Tupin' had gone triple platinum in the U.S.

Damn, those were the days. No TikTok or Facebay then, thank Christ.'

The band all laughed, having learned of Kilo's massive success in the 80s and 90s managing country and western artistes across the states—a veritable gold mine, even today. They were sure he'd seen the sights, to say the least.

Dom made a request. 'Kilo, can we arrange for you to hang out with us or come for a drink sometime? I'm sure you've got lots of advice and funny stories. Also, thanks. By the way, not having to deal with the band's e-mails and socials has been great. I can actually write songs, have hobbies' she smiled.

'Hobbies? Yeah, sure, Dominica. I'll make sure we do that soon. Just you guys keep workin' hard. We're gonna get there, believe me. Now I ain't ever been to Sweden, but it looks like my kinda place.' He knelt down a little to look out of the window.

'Lots of lakes and little ranch-type a things. I'm booked into a nature spa place tonight. Probably get my ass whipped by a birch branch... in a white toga dress.'

He laughed and winked at the band, all rather bewildered by his being. 'Well done though, guys, seriously. Remember to be at the venue before stage time. And try some of those Swedish meatballs, yeah? You look like you need a shower, too.'

He sauntered off the bus giving Tubo a high five. He seemed to wear a different plaid shirt every day; Nick noticed. He'd taken to view Kilo in a cartoon-like light. He was unfazed by everything, this guy—a real rodeo rebel.

The bus engines roared up, and they cruised along the Swedish motorways, taking turns to play songs and try some potent Grapefruit Radler they'd picked up. Nick liked to take some time to himself on tour, so he eventually retreated to his bunk and left Ana to toil on her book assignments. Dom and Cammie were sprawled out on the couches.

Nick liked to double-check all of his prescriptions were in the right bag compartments. His guitar hadn't moved, and his handful of belongings was placed exactly where they should be. He swallowed a couple of his meds and lay in his bunk, strumming a chord sequence he'd been excited about since it came to him. He'd heard a bass part and piano melody in his head. He couldn't wait to record it. He was also loving playing all the new material live, as was Dom. She seemed to be taking her place as frontwoman with gusto. Her voice sounded better than ever. They just had to find a way to swim against the tides and keep the good ship afloat.

Nick had noticed a slight tremor in his hands for the past few days, though he had put it down to stage nerves. It could, in the sober light of day, be a physical reaction to the lack of chemicals in his system. He didn't mention it to the band. There was too much going on; that much was certain.

Dark purple, then bright yellow and pure white fields shimmered past the window at a hypnotic pace. Sweden harbored a subtly beauty; hikers, windmills, and Nordic charm. What Nick imagined Switzerland mixed with Finland might be like. He popped another tablet and slowly felt his anxieties decrease. He took in the array of multicoloured flower pods, all at varying expansions in their cycles. The trickling of freshwater streams outside calmed into a trippy stupor. The bus was silent for once, and he slept for hours...

18

'Get up. It's seven o'clock. Nick!'

Nick jumped up in his bunk with fright, the blue neon lights illuminating his face in the dark of the bunk.

'We're on in an hour.'

Dom and Cammie had changed their clothes and were looking a little drunk, laughing at the sound of Morrissey over the tour bus stereo.

'Heaven knows we're in Sweden now,' muttered Nick, climbing out of the bunk and grabbing an open bottle of beer. 'How long was I out for? And where's Ana?'

'She's gone to get food with Tubo and the kung fu guy. You slept about six hours dude. Must have been yesterday's drama.' Cammie took a swig from a half bottle of unrecognisable spirits, passing it to Nick, who braved a slug. He coughed violently and tried not to spit it out. 'What the hell is that, Cammie? Tastes like moonshine.'

'What's moonshine?. It's local sleigh Gin. I've no idea what percentage it is. Hey, Dom and I were on those massage seats at the gas station. One euro. They're incredible. I feel like a new man.'

'Yeah, they saved me a few times on our first tour, Cammie. I wouldn't recommend it on a comedown, mind.'

The trio laughed, and 'This Charming Man' burst onto the stereo. 'Let's gooo,' shouted Dom. It was almost showtime. Ana and the crew got back on the bus and looked at the band expectantly. 'Hey guys, you know, from outside the venue there's about five thousand people partying and shouting.'

'Really?' said Dom. 'Oh wow.'

'I've just woken up, Ana. I'm gonna have a heart attack,' joked Nick unconvincingly. Ana handed him a salad bowl and a jet-black triple espresso. 'This probably won't help, then.'

Cammie opened two bottles of champagne. He passed them all a tiny pill and put his bag back on his bunk.

'What's this, Cammie?' said Nick and Dom, slightly perplexed by the offer. Weren't they avoiding this on tour from now on?

'Don't worry. It's legal. Well, it's not illegal. It's a thing my guy in New York gave me. I got over a hundred. It's a hybrid of performance-enhancing substances. It enriches the brain but also gives the effect of mild ecstasy. It's amazing.'

Nick and Dom shrugged their shoulders and washed them down with the 700 krone a-pop bottles of bubbles. Luckily, they figured out it was around fifty pounds. Their budget was growing considerably, nonetheless.

The band jumped and hugged at the side of the stage, having raided most of the tour bus rider. They felt giddy-drunk, ready to take on the world, a trio of hyperactive heartbeats and alcoholic fuzz.

The crowd was getting ravenous now, all screams and flying glow sticks. They all took a deep breath and strolled out, one by one.

The cameras started like a swarm of tiny, blinding bulbs. The atmosphere exploded in applause. The ground shook, readying itself for a storm. They were ready to take Sweden one hit at a time, and cherished every spine-tingling, rib-quacking second of it. Cammie's addition of uppers had the desired effect, and he was rolling off extra drum solos. Dom gyrated and slashed his bass-drum skin with her bass between harmony breaks. Another city down, no hiccups. Not on stage, anyway.

'How many times, Nick, honestly you've got to watch out. I'm not coming to A+E like the last tour. I told you already. I'm not a nurse.'

Nick was lying on his bunk, nursing a cut lip and smashed knuckle. He'd thrown his guitar against his amp at the end of their last song, taken a ten-foot volley into the front rows, and surfed his way halfway across the venue. The injuries were a minor setback, for the crowd had been electric.

Dom herself had considered the feat, but with a growing number of fans and possible gropers in the audience, she no longer enjoyed jumping into crowds.

The band sat in a rather plush Malmö motor stop, nursing a combo of migraines and memories. As always, they tried out some Swedish snacks like Cinnamon Gifflar and mini croustades, like a sweetbread tartlet combo. They sauntered back to the tour bus, knowing there were more press junkets to attend to. Tubo was waiting for them, gorging on a choco roll at the back. 'Mr. Cecil wants to talk,' he said, spinning his open laptop around.

'Good morning,' he said over a slightly hazy screen. He was filing a nail. The Barcelona skyline shone in the background.

'The situation is under control. I am doing all I can to deal with the Pachos. And the Brothers Black are back in Spain, I've learned.'

A woman in a black bra walked past in the background. Tubo laughed.

'I got some other news for you. So you know this band, Ze Conks? I have dropped them off the label. In fact, I should kick their asses back to Bradford.'

He went on. 'I let them record on the Scottish island, at the Barn, Fazio's old place.' 'Yeah, we know the place, said Nick. 'We know the people. It's grand,' said Nick.

'Yeah, well, anyways. The band was being idiots, completa dummies. They tell me they want 'artistic freedom' on the phone. They send me a pile of shit CD that sounds like Pink Floyd being played backwards. They are taking far too many hippie drugs. But then, then I find out they have been causing all sorts of problems in a café there. A bar, whatever.'

'A bar? What, Johannes little pub? Hahaha! What happened there?' shrieked Dom. They were all paying close attention as the story unravelled.

'The singer, this skinny guy that thinks he's David Bowie or something, was blindly drunk one night and tried to kick the owner's dog, urinated on himself and started a fight with two fishermen. She took photos of it all and sold them to a newspaper to get revenge. The Sun or something. The band has imploded. The singer threatened to sue the island and was taken to a hospital in a gold dressing gown. So I had to let them go.'

The band had erupted in laughter; shouts of 'Go Joanne!' further confusing Don Cechil.

'Fucking hippies, these guys. Anyway, I got to go. Keep making those hits, folks. Adios.'

The line went dead. The band was simply in the wonder of The Conks' stupidity. Poor guys probably wouldn't sing on a pre-written hit ever again.

'Shit, that's even better than some of my industry stories,' laughed Cammie. 'I'm gonna e-mail Joanne. I hope she got a lot for the pictures!' They all laughed some more, equally relieved they wouldn't be sharing a stage with the band over the summer. Johnny Jah would have to go back to auditioning for reality TV with burnt nostrils. They did feel for the band, nonetheless.

They got some music on, and Tubo took the driver's seat for another fourteen hours on the road. The ju-jitsu enthusiast was eating his way through bags of dried fruit and reading books. They were happy he was there, even if reluctant to chat.

Another day of online interviews and Q&A's beckoned, then on to Finland and Poland, new territory for the band. Dom had been desperate to see the Northern lights for most of her life, so was hoping this might be her chance.

'So you guys wanna talk, huh? Here I am. I ain't had time, dealing with those guys, The Conks. Tragic, but anyways...'

Kilo sat on their bus with an iced tea, looking suitably refreshed after his Swedish spa experience. 'Hot Stones, man,' he winked at the band.

They'd left Sweden and were over the border to Finland, with Kilo joining them for a few hours. They got to chatting about Kilo's history, his life story even, having grown up in Dallas and obsessing over Country ballads. His plan was to buy a vast ranch and retire after he'd made good with the band.

'Believe it or not, I started out in Journalism. I worked for the Dallas Explorer and ran a music fanzine on the side, mostly country and folk stuff. I played guitar as a session player too. Hey Nick I noticed you got a nice Martin DX-2, I'd keep a hold of that if I were you. No javelin with that beauty. Anyways, then I got married and used my contacts to start management, with country pop acts, and worked my way up.

Lots of people have no idea quit how big and far-reaching this music is, not just in the U.S. You got Australia, Canada. You know who Carrie Underwood is?'

The band shrugged their shoulders.

'Probably sold more records than the Beatles. But I'm kinda peripatetic, always moving around, so it suited me. And this thing I do,' Kilo ran his hand down his jacket. 'You might like to call it an act, it's just a persona. I find it easier not to be taken too seriously. But I know what I'm doin', aint no charlatan. Take a look at my bank balance if you like.'

The band felt they understood Kilo a little better now, probably having underestimated his cunning.

'I am a veritable gent, at the end of the day, which is very rare in this industry, let me tell you that. And I don't feel satisfied until I've squeezed every drop of success out of my artistes. Hence why I'm one of the best in the business.' Kilo looked out of the window and cracked a knuckle.

'I done seen it all - decadence and decline, kids. Tantrums and platinum trophies. You know, nowadays, I tend to just laugh about most things. It's important to have a sense of humour in this game. Otherwise, you'll either cry or wind up snortin' weed killer, ya hear?'

He cackled and gave Dom, who was finding him comical, a subtle elbow nudge. Cammie felt he could relate to much of Kilo's outlook, having himself dealt with all manner of fragile egos, or esteemed rappers. He could see why some form of persona in the music industry was like armour.

The album had become a success all over Europe and the UK. Soon, they'd start their onslaught of world domination in the U.S.

'You guys should be celebrating. You've almost paid off Ceceel, and you're gonna see the world. Tomorrow you got a trip to try and see the Northern Lights. I thought y'all could probably use a break.'

'Really? Fantastic!' went Dom. Nick and Cammie both smiled too. Kilo sipped his iced tea. A new plaid shirt: khaki and cherry today.

'Before I forget, here's your schedule. Tomorrow's day off. I booked hotels, figured you guys need a break. Then two big outdoor festivals, on alpine resorts. We finish up in Poland, Czech, and then the U.K, then back to Madrid, Barcelona.'

'Hey,' shrieked Cammie, staring at his phone, 'I got an e-mail reply from Joanne.'

'Who the heck's Joanne?' barked Kilo, confused.

'It's a long story Kilo. She's an inspiration.' Nick and Dom were leaning forward in anticipation. Cammie read aloud.

Dear Brothers and Sisters,

I hope your European tour is a success. The show I saw with my daughter was fantastic. And Nick, I can't believe you released the song in my name as a single. It warms my heart so much.

Here everything is fine. Mr. Finn is always asking after you. We had a bit of bother with some new people, a band called The Conks. They were recording up at the barn. They were acting like absolute tearaways. Their singer managed to upset most of the Island – fights not withstanding. Anyway, after he kicked Dino, I took revenge with my Camera, and my daughter got me £4000 from The Sun Newspaper. He was uncontrollable, trying to re-enact some sort of Syd Barrett circus act.

Hope to see you all soon. Ps. I bought a second dog with the money!

Big Hugs, Joanne x

The band could see the landscape changing yet again through the bus window. The sun was going down. Here it was: the icy splendour of Finland. Mountains of melting snow cascaded past the bus windows. Though it was summer, a crisp bite hung in the air. It reminded Nick of Edinburgh.

'Isn't this the happiest country in the world?' noted Dom.

'There's hope for you yet, Nick,' sniggered Cammie, taking in the cloudless sky.

'Piss off, eh. Aren't the Moomins from Finland?'

'Yeah. So are Glass Igloos and Salamakki Candies,' added Ana. 'We'll get some at the next pit stop…'

The bus tore through the lakes and never-ending forests, up into the city of Helsinki, where the band would be playing an outdoor festival before a brief break. They took to their bunks one by one, making random chat to one another in the dark.

'I think that Kilo is actually quite a decent guy. When he drops the persona thing.'

Ana was blowing breath clouds against the window next to Nick.

'Yeah' shouted Dom from her bunk. 'At least he's down the line. No bullshit.'

'He's funny. The man's care free.' added Cammie, vaping clouds of Cola smoke into the bus walkway. 'Looks like a limo tailpipe ignited up there Cammie.'

'Whatever, Nick. Get your long johns on'.

Cammie gazed out of his window at the stark, lonely Finnish landscape. Unfrequented but remarkable, nonetheless. His arms ached from the daily pounding of drums. Tearing of t-shirts. Amid the jokes and frovilities, he suddenly felt, for the first time, aeons from home. With this sadness came a distant light; the warmth of stage lights and spine-sugaring roar of a crowd.

Nick grabbed his acoustic and played around with a riff that had come into his head after his sleep. He wasn't sure why that happened, but it did. He sometimes felt like he knew how someone like Brian Wilson, Bjork or Quincy Jones operated. Bells would start playing notes, sometimes harpsichords or cellos, around his brain. It could be anything really. Triggered by the merest of sounds, sights. He somehow managed to get some on to records, some not.

They all shared a strip of Temazepam and slowly drifted off.

The Scandi saga continued.

19

'Dom! Can we have a photo for Insta? Please.'

The band was wading through a small gaggle of fans trying to get into the artiste's area of Open Air Anarchy, a Finnish fest combining snowboarding and music. The backdrop was remarkable: a huge sloping hill that enabled tens of thousands of music fans to enjoy alpine sports in their free time. Or guzzling Alka Seltzer on ski lifts.

'Cammie,' shouted a female voice out of the twenty or so fans. It was teeming and tight, but the band always took the time to sign caps or hug their fans.

Cammie was standing beside a group of girls, three iPhones zapping at his grinning face.

Suddenly, he felt an enormous thud and simultaneous sting in his cheek before losing sight in one eye. It reminded him of being pummeled by a brand new leather ball at school. He couldn't breathe, his limbs went soft, and he could hear screams around him. A fist had flown out of nowhere and landed on his cheek, almost knocking him unconscious. A fracas of security, including Ju-Jitsu man, scampered around the band. The assailant had darted off rapidly, leaving pockets of space among the crowds. He was nowhere to be seen.

'Jeez – you OK, Cammie?' shouted Dom, helping him to his feet. He had a cut on his cheek, like a segment of strawberry stuck to his fizzog. Nick cradled his arm. Ju-Jitsu was fuming. A bewildered Ana held onto Tubo's log-sized arm.

'I'm OK,' he shouted. 'What the hell was that?' They'd been

moved without even noticing. The others and Ana were swiftly ushered into a Porta Cabin backstage.

Droplets of blood ran down his right cheek, which Dom dabbed with a towel.

'I saw him. He's with the Pachos. I caught a look at his tattoo, their symbol.'

They all turned to face Ju-Jitsu.

'Do you speak English?' asked Ana. The man looked at them all, still aggravated by the furore.

'Not always. Sometimes I have to. My name's Tom. Call me T.'

'Mr. T,' joked Cammie, making light of his reddening shirt collar.

'Don't worry guys. It's a ski festival. I'll wear a Bandana. Probably look pretty cool anyway. I need some more of that Finish Jaloviina brandy.'

The band was huddled around the side of the stage for their late afternoon slot. Nick was shaking a little and took a swig of a black bottle of Koskenkorva, soon realising it was larynx-shredding Finnish vodka. Ideal to heat up the chest, the band figured.

Cammie was looking out over the huge crowd and the magnificent mountain backdrop. He'd managed to source a blue bandana from a fan and matched it with a bright white t-shirt, like a Finnish flag bearer. Ana, Tubo, and T were up high in the steel rafters, taking in the sun-soaked icy panorama and chatting.

Dom took a last swig of the Vodka and jumped on the spot. A local Snowboarding champ was introducing the band now. Nick grabbed the bottle, feeling good after the band had scooped two of Cammies mysterious super-caplets each. They walked on.

A huge roar met the band, all feeling energised, and Cammie's nerves battled with the bandana, causing him a slight fit of hyperventilation. Dom had snatched her Bass and was pacing more than usual, her purple streak flashing towards Nick. He knew she was mad. This would be a wild one, Nick thought. He knew Dom inside out.

'Hello Finland,' shouted Dom after the first song, flares, snowballs, and drinks cups spattering the crowds like an Alpine food fight. Nick was gearing up for one of their new singles, he plucked the opening riff, and Cammie and Dom tore into it in perfect synergy. Dom kicked her amp, followed by a cup that flew straight back into the crowd. She was feral, buzzing.

As Nick sang the first chorus, he looked onto the horizon over the swarming heat of the crowd. The cool air had produced clouds of condensation over the crowd's heads.

Suddenly, he noticed a large black flag bearing the symbol of the Pachos logo. The same one he'd seen the Brothers Black do with their hands before. He tried to concentrate on singing, moving his head up toward Ana and T up in the metallic stage frame. Dom was staring at Cammie between backing vocals, nodding toward the flag. He caught sight of Ana pointing the flag out to T. Nick was overcome with anger. They'd disrespected his fiancé, done away with her uncle, and beat up his drummer. He ran three steps and kicked his fuzz pedal against the amp like a drunken penalty kick. He smashed his guitar on the ground, splinters of wood and plastic burst into the air. He made it back to the mic for the chorus. Suddenly, Nick watched T bound from the structure above and leap onto the stage.

As he continued singing, T did a running dive-bomb straight into the front row of the huge crowd, who roared at what they assumed was an exuberant stage diver. The band watched T's t-shirt being ripped off his back as he surfed over a sea of hands toward the flag. He was almost upside down, and one stray leg was all that was on show as the song reached its climax—a mammoth moshpit of jumping bodies everywhere. Cammie could feel the sting of sweat drops slowly entering his cut. Around ten seconds later, with the band bursting with adrenaline and thudding cerebrums, the flag suddenly disappeared.

They all exchanged glances. Mr. T had found the culprits, whoever they were...

'Hurry up, Dom, Cammie, the boat's gonna leave!' The band was power-walking toward a late afternoon Seacruiser to try and catch the Aurora Borealis. Tubo and T were up front, Tubo trying his hardest to fit through the narrow entrance of the vessel.

It'd been a hectic day. Kilo had booked them in for the excursion and a plush hotel after. He himself was busy being dunked into an ice pond by a Finnish physician for healing.

'So what happened, T? We thought we'd lost you there, out in the crowd.' The band was popping on their miniature seatbelts, waiting to set sail, turbo style.

'Lose me? No way. I found the guy. Listen to this, kids. He was one of Pachos' men, of course. Not one of the Brothers, but still, almost as good. I got him and struck a Judo chop to his neck. He went down like a sack of Moldovan spuds.' The band was listening closely as the story unravelled. Having heard the story already, Tubo was chortling loudly, scoffing a packet of salmon slices. Cammie joined him, although his cheek hurt every time he attempted a laugh.

'I saw, up ahead, a ski lift going to the mountain. I had to take advantage of the tools I was dealt with. So, I marched his limp body up to the ski lift. A really old 1970s swing thing. When it came round, I dumped him on the seat and got on with him.'
'No – so what did you do to him?' Ana was getting upset. Even Nick and Dom were fearing the worst, now.

'Nothing really. I was in a good mood. But as we went up, taking in the nice scenery, I took the flag he had been waving and wrapped it round his body. He was still out cold, the sadsack. Then as we ascended to the peak, I took my phone out. I took a picture of his limp edifice, tied to the ski lift, with only one sock on. In fact, I took about seven photos. I made sure the Pachos flag was waving in the wind. I sent them immediately to your Uncle Cechil and hopped off at the top, I got back to the festival on time to hitch a ride from Tubo.' The band was cracking up; feeling a shared sense of retribution had won the day.

'So, where's the guy now?' asked Nick. He'd had enough cruelty for one day. 'Well, he'll have woken up on the ski lift, mostly naked. The great 'Veganza!' as your uncle would say.' He winked at Ana.

'Damn right, bro, I even chipped a tooth' muttered Cammie.

The boat set off through the bitter Nordic waters, and the band requested a bottle of Reyka to share. After two hours of deranged dolphin spotting and a seaboard spin of Belle and Sebastian, the boat suddenly stopped as the sun set. A cabin crew lady who had been serving them tit-bits of Finnish cuisine approached, looking animated.

'If you would like to come to the front of the boat, our other guests are taking in the lights.'

Cammie and Dom were snuggled into a cocoon, sharing a woollen cardi to stay warm. Dom opened an eye and leapt up, wide awake. 'The lights! The Aurora Borealis!'

She jumped up and leaped into the ship's narrow pathway, knocking Tubo's hot dog out of his hand. She was out the door in seconds. Onions had spattered a passenger's hair in front. The band and T followed, with Tubo coming up the rear, muttering and sliding sauce from his chin. And there it was: the magical green glory of the northern lights. Like an explosion of emerald particles and smoke trails made of apple green, it was spellbinding. Nick and Ana held hands, with Dom and Cammie latching arms. Even Tubo and T seemed to be speechless. 'Wow,' said Dom. 'You've no idea how special this is for me.' The band was slowly pirouetting in circles, staring vertically at the sky. Dom handed Tubo her phone, ensuring he got at least ten snaps of the band together, smiling under the northern lights. Nick and Ana, and unexpectedly, she and Cammie, she insisted. Cammie was looking rather chirpy at the suggestion, even blushing a little. Nick didn't think he'd ever seen Dom look so happy, so calmly content. They all huddled together at the ship's bow and shared sips of the Reyka, bathed in the emerald heavens.

20

'Nick, can you get a move on? We're going to be late for the meeting.'

'Aye, hold on. I don't know where to put these clothes.' Nick was rummaging around, banging into plants, and arranging his new souvenirs. He threw a pair of loafers onto a pile.

'You know, when I was broke, I used to save for a pair of Converse. Nowadays, I'm getting sent bundles of designer jackets. The latest everything. Isn't life ridiculous, eh?' shouted Nick, through the doorway.

'Well, the rich get richer,' added Ana, bemused.

They were back in their Barcelona apartment, unpacking from the six-week tour. It'd been a rollercoaster, and the band was nearing exhaustion.

Cammie had a newly-acquired staved arm, Nick had lost ten pounds, and Dom had written three new songs, so not all was lost.

'Yes, well, Uncle Cechil and Kilo will be there soon. We can't keep them waiting.'

'All right, I'm ready. Where are we going anyway?'

Nick blew out a plume of acrid smoke from his camel.

'It's a tiny, furtive café. My uncle is completely paranoid. He's showing signs of a minor meltdown. I don't know what he's been doing.'

'I wonder, eh'. Nick cleared his nose and continued packing. 'Probably not working on an oganic farm.'

They met Cammie and Dom on the sidewalk and caught a cab to Café Las Rive.

Nick was already dreading the flight to America, his anxiety levels had been slowly creeping up, but he stayed quiet, bit his nails, and took his tablets.

The band arrived and had to walk down a narrow alleyway around three feet wide, peppered with Spanish trinkets from the rafters.

They entered a dark doorway and saw Kilo sitting alone with a Bourbon at the table. It was considerably more lavish than they'd expected, although dark, candle-lit.

'Hey,' he hollered, in his brash Texan twang. 'If it isn't ABBA.'

The band mostly winced and got seated. 'You guys look like anaemic peasants.'

'Thanks, Kilo. Hopefully, you're enjoying your time with us,' came Dom's response, with a sarcastic smirk. 'Cheeky,' sighed Cammie, nursing his arm.

'Well, you gotta roll with the punches. You guys got a week off anyway. At least try to look happy. This isn't a Smiths convention.'

Nick had to laugh. Kilo was sharp. Suddenly two men appeared in the room, Don Cecil's burly aides, bouncers, whatever they were. The man himself stalked along the alleyway in a long black coat and hat. They could see him through the windows.

'Hello, people,' he announced, entering the room. More of his men were placed along the passageway.

'Hi there, Mr.Ceceeel,' said Kilo. 'We been waitin' for you.'

Don got seated at the head of the table and was brought two espressos by an aide, not a waitress.

'I've got some news for you all. Firstly, the album has been a runaway success. Everything is moving in the right direction. Next, we are taking America, one state at a time.'

The band looked on in contemplation, balls of worry and wishful wonder.

'You have done well in the past six months. Yes. And also, I've got a funny story to tell you. Regarding our little problem, The Black Brothers and co.'

He took off his hat and, stroking his shirt at the collar, snorted.

'Unfortunately, Mr. Pacho is still out there. We are looking to deal with that. But in the meantime, this is a tale my brother would have been proud of, my dearest Fazio.'

Don gulped down a whole espresso and patted his mouth with a napkin.

The band were all staring at him, battered and bruised but psyched to have a week off.

'So we caught the Black Brothers. They have started a new life. My men were making a shipment, of multivitamins, to an island off Panama.'

'Multivitamins, huh?' whispered Kilo to Cammie. Both tried not to laugh.

'So they dumped them there. On an island with sixty-five inhabitants.'

Don went on, looking pleased with himself.

'Before they left, I got a picture of the two covered in pig excrement. Anyway, then, then I found out their boss—Mr. Pacho—was attending a grand, selected production at Liceu Opera House.'

He began to smile. Mr. T was at the doorway now. He'd

joined the group. He'd smiled for once. Don gave him a nod.

'I realised the sound engineer at the Opera was one of my staff. He helps do videos and production for my artistes.'

'So I called him and had him make the Grande unveiling. He displayed the two pictures—the ones of our friend in the Alps, taken by Mr. T, and the one of the Black Brothers, smelling divine—on a huge projector screen at the start of the Opera, for thirty seconds.'

They all began to laugh, one by one, some awkwardly, some proudly, and Kilo downright baffled.

'Mr. Pacho had to sit with his wife, surrounded by his men, red-faced and seething, for the next three hours.'

Don inhaled his second espresso. He dabbed his mouth and motioned to his men.

'I'm sorry, but I must be on my way. I have to keep on the move. I am incognito yet again. I do hope you all enjoy America. I wouldn't. Ana, I will be in touch with you. We have to discuss our moves to the future. And Kilo here has arranged your trip. Travel, stays, everything.'

He got up and took shook Ana's hand, bowing his head. His men and Ju-jitsu followed.

'Now, just hold on a second, Mr. Ceceeel,' shouted Kilo. He gulped his Bourbon and stood up. A stool fell over. 'I hope you done paid me half my loot. I'm goin' to Reno when I get back home. Shoot me some slot machines, ya hear?'

Don smirked, turning around.

'Hush now, Kilo. You have been wired your pocket money. Now go and fetch me more mullah, you mook.'

Don exited and paced down the alleyway, twiddling a cufflink with one hand. He really did look like a senior Nostra today. A sinister smirk beneath gunmetal grey stubble.

His men followed.

'Well, I'll be damned,' said Kilo, his voice had moved up an octave. 'Who wants a drink, then?'

Nick, Ana, Dom, and Cammie all bundled out into the street an hour later. The signs of city life thrust them back to reality. Las Ramblas Blvd was bustling with tourists, clattering café spoons, and traffic.

'Hold on, guys. I'm just going to Bankomat.' Nick was rummaging around between euros, pounds, and plectrums.

'So, what are your plans for your week off, Dom?' Ana inquired. The midday sun was like a warming face mask.

'Well, now that you ask, erm, Cammie's actually booked something for us together. So, I don't know, is the answer.'

'Really? OK, well, great. I guess we'll have to find out later.'

Ana smiled at Dom, and Cammie stared awkwardly in a different direction.

'Hey, you guys,' said Nick, standing with his back to the group.

'Has anyone actually checked their bank balance recently?'

'Nah, I'm too scared,' mumbled Dom.

'Well, I think you probably should, Dominica. I'm going into the bank.'

Nick took Ana's hand.

'How come?'

'If my math is correct, judging by what I had last month, Don's given us £135k each.'

'What, are you joking? For this last tour?'

'Yup. Well, i think that's what it's for..' Nick paused, puzzled, glinting at the bright city sky.

'So, I'm going to send my mum twenty. She can take the whole family on holiday. Whatever she wants. Plus, Ana and I have a wedding to plan.'

'That's amazing, Nick,' exclaimed Cammie. 'You know, I might just do the same - I've been missin' my moms too.'

'Hundred percent,' smiled Dom. 'Let's get in there.'

They filed into a single line at the bureau de change with mixed mushes of cheesy grins. The suited clerks didn't seem too enamoured with them. A radio cackled in the background. Nick sang along, as if by second nature.

'And I know-oow / It's only rock n roll.' The clerks all stared. Confused, unimpressed by this gaggle of oddly paired ruffians. Dom picked up on the song, and in a burst of telepathy, finished up:

'Its only rock n roll, but I like it!'

THE END